I0592507

FIRE IN THE VINEYARD

The Wine Lover's Daughter, Book Three

ALSO BY CHRISTA POLKINHORN

NOVELS

The Italian Sister
The Wine Lover's Daughter, Book One

Finding Angelo
The Wine Lover's Daughter, Book Two

An Uncommon Family
Family Portrait, Book One

Love of a Stonemason
Family Portrait, Book Two

Emilia
Family Portrait, Book Three

POETRY

Path of Fire

FIRE IN THE VINEYARD

The Wine Lover's Daughter, Book Three

Christa Polkinhorn

Bookworm Press

Bookworm Press
1223 Wilshire Blvd., #1054
Santa Monica, CA 90403

Copyright © 2018 by Christa Polkinhorn

All rights reserved. No part of this publication may be reproduced in any form or by any means (electronic, mechanical, photocopying, recording, or otherwise) without the prior written permission of the copyright owner, excepting brief excerpts used in reviews.

This is a work of fiction. Names, characters, places, and incidents are either the product of the author's imagination or are used fictitiously. Any resemblance to actual events or persons, living or dead, is entirely coincidental.

Cover design: Diane Busch
Cover images: iStock, Andreas Saldavs

ISBN: 978-0-9600135-0-0

Printed in the United States of America

In Memory of Bernard Lauer

Prologue

"So, where is that gambler you talked about?" George Winter asked, glancing at his watch.

"He'll show up. No worries," Anton said.

The two friends were sitting at a table on the patio of a bar in San Luis Obispo in California's Central Coast region, drinking beer. George removed his baseball cap and wiped the sweat from his forehead, then put it back on.

It was a warm and muggy day in March. Dark ominous-looking clouds had gathered in the west. George took a sip of beer, then glanced at the creek in the ravine below the patio. A sudden gust of wind brushed through the trees, making the leaves of the silver birches tremble. The breeze felt invigorating, but almost immediately the oppressive air rushed back. From inside the bar, the clashing of dishes and occasional shouts could be heard.

"Is it going to rain?" George gazed at the sky, then looked down at the creek. Heaps of rotted leaves from the trees that had accumulated in the shallow water gave off a musty smell.

"Sure could use it. This drought sucks big time," Anton said. "Hey, that's him!" He waved at someone behind George and called out, "The master gambler."

George turned around and watched a man step out of the bar onto the patio. He was middle-aged, of medium height, slim and wiry, with sculpted facial features. His dark, curly hair, tinted with gray, was combed back from his face. An overall modest, clean appearance, George felt. The most striking feature was his dark eyes with which he quickly scanned his environment with a guarded look.

"Never was a master," the man said with a low, dark voice.

"Oh, really?" George observed him curiously, then got up. Anton slapped the man on the back, and George shook hands with him. The man's hand was long, narrow, and firm. George noticed he wore a small cross on a silver chain around his neck. He motioned the guest to sit down. "Would you like a beer or something else?"

The man pulled up a chair. "Corona, please," he said to the waitress who had joined them. George and Anton reordered Bud Lights.

"I'm George," Winter introduced himself while waiting for their drinks.

"Norman," the man said after a brief pause as if he hesitated to give his identity away.

After the waitress brought their drinks, the men took a few sips of beer. George measured the man quizzically, then put his glass down.

"I'm looking for someone to join our small group of card players—poker and some other games," George said.

Norman shook his head. "I don't gamble anymore."

"Oh, it's not really gambling. It's just card games between friends. We sometimes play for small amounts of money, nothing major. Just a private gathering at my place. Completely legal."

Norman shot him a cautious glance. "Maybe. I'll think about it."

"Norman is your real name?" George winked.

The man named Norman shrugged. "It was my gambling name."

"Ah, no problem. As long as the money you play with is real." George chuckled.

"What makes you so sure you'll get any money from me?" Norman raised an eyebrow, then cracked a quick smile. "Don't worry. The money is real."

"Where have you gambled?" George asked.

Norman shrugged. "Different places, here and abroad."

George was intrigued by this newcomer. He tried to draw him out, find out more about his personal life. Norman was quiet, polite, and mysterious and didn't give anything away. George called the waiter and ordered another round. He hoped to make some money, which he sorely needed after spending time in prison. He couldn't find a regular job, but he had begun what looked like a profitable venture in the wine business together with a few friends. For this, however, he needed extra cash. He had gambled in the past, just for a little money, and had often won. Somehow, he felt this new guy could help him win more. It was worth a try.

Chapter 1

"Dad, where are you going?" Matthew Segantino said as he stepped into his father's office and spotted the suitcase next to the desk. Then he remembered. "Oh, yes, Spain." He tried to suppress his irritation. *There he goes again.*

Robert Segantino, owner of the famed Segantino Winery in Paso Robles, California, was off to another blind wine-tasting event, this time in Madrid. California wines had won several gold and silver medals a few years before, and Robert decided to submit his Syrah at this year's contest. He also planned to visit some of his most important clients in Europe.

"Dad, I really need to talk to you about the plans for the cellar. I need—"

"Not now, Matt. Just go on with the planning. We'll talk when I'm back." Robert got up and raked his fingers through his short curly hair. His dark, almost black eyes expressed impatience. He was of medium height, somewhat stocky without being fat, dressed in black jeans and a button-down shirt.

Matthew sighed. "I've planned it all, but I can't really complete anything without your consent."

Robert grabbed his suitcase. "Do whatever you can, and we'll discuss it later. You can organize a lot without me being involved."

"Not really," Matthew said. "I can't hire musicians for instance without offering them a fee, and that I can't do without you."

"Then wait with this and do the other stuff."

"Such as?" Matthew felt a spike of anger and clenched his jaw. He'd had these kinds of arguments with his father a lot lately.

"Such as?" His father's voice rose. "Jesus, Matt, show some initiative."

Matthew's face grew hot. He felt like blowing up but checked himself and exhaled deeply. He knew it was useless. His dad was on the point of leaving and wasn't interested in any complaints from his son. "Okay. Whatever. Do you need a ride to the airport?"

"No. Mom is doing that." Robert walked outside.

Matthew followed him. "I thought she was going with you?"

"She backed out. She said she was getting tired of these wine tasting events."

"Don't blame her," Matthew muttered under his breath. He, too, was tired of his father traveling all over the globe. He wished he'd stay put once in a while, so they could have a meaningful working relationship. Matthew had a lot of ideas but couldn't put them into practice because his father still had complete authority over the running of the winery and the estate. He didn't object to Matthew's ideas, but he had to give his signature for any financial transaction or organizational changes.

Matthew's mother waved at him as she drove up in their Jeep, then got out of the car and greeted him with a kiss while his father put his suitcase on the back seat.

"Not going to Spain?" Matthew asked.

Janice, a middle-aged, slender, attractive woman with short wavy blond hair and green-blue eyes, raised an eyebrow and gave a quick smile. "No, I decided to visit a friend nearby instead. I'm getting fed up with these long-distance plane trips." She got back into the car and waved once more.

Matthew watched his parents drive away, then turned around and let his eyes wander over their vast estate. Huge fields of symmetrically planted vines covered the rolling hills and the valleys. He heard the sputtering sound of a farm vehicle nearby. Behind him, overlooking their property from a hill, was his parents' home, a large house in the Tuscan style with yellow-beige walls and green wooden trim. It was a beautiful home. Matthew lived in a guesthouse in the same style next to it. He was able to live there rent-free and only had to pay for the utilities and upkeep. This was a big help, since he was paying off his substantial student loan from his studies in viticulture and enology at the University of California, Davis.

It was a crisp, cool day in May. Matthew inhaled the light scent of sagebrush mixed with the sweet smell of lilacs in his parents' garden. It had rained a little in February and March, so the hills and valleys were still green. Unfortunately, the rain wasn't enough to make a dent in the many years of drought in California.

Matthew walked the short distance to his grandparents' part of the property. Years ago, his father and grandfather had split their estate. His grandfather had kept the smaller part, three of his favorite varietals, the Italian Sangiovese, Nebbiolo, and Aglianico grapes. Now, they belonged to his brother Nicholas Segantino and his wife Sofia. Matthew stopped next to a field of Sangiovese grapes and walked along one of the rows of vines. The fruit was abundant and looked healthy. He squinted in the bright midday sun and scanned the four grape fields that belonged to his brother.

Sometimes, he envied Nicholas who, because of the smaller size of his property and the help of his wife Sofia and

Grandfather Martin, was able to do a lot of the hands-on work himself, such as planting and caring for the vines and harvesting the grapes. Robert's estate, which Matthew and Nadia, his sister, who was still studying at UC Davis, would inherit one day, was so large that it required quite a few employees. There wasn't much time for Matthew to work in the vineyards and the cellar, something he had always enjoyed. Now, the actual manual work was done by the staff, and he was mainly responsible for the organizational part. He didn't mind, he liked to organize things, but he sometimes missed the "getting-your-hands-dirty" kind of work, as his grandfather called it.

Matthew arrived at his grandparents' home, a medium-size wooden cottage, much smaller than his parents' house, but Matthew loved its rustic and homey style. Just when he was about to use the brass grapevine knocker, the door opened. His grandfather, Martin Segantino, a tall, skinny man with short white hair and brown eyes, smiled at him.

"Hey there, Matt. Come on in. Nice to see you. You guys must be busy." He stepped outside and checked the mailbox.

As Matthew joined his grandparents and his brother and sister-in-law in the living room, he inhaled the faint smell of tomato sauce that wafted from the kitchen.

"Yeah, all kinds of stuff is going on." Matthew plopped himself on the sofa next to Sofia and Nicholas. He pointed to Sofia's belly. "How's my favorite nephew doing in there?"

Sofia grinned. "Getting heavy. Definitely a boy." She patted the bulge. "We're at eight months now."

"Well, Matt, you missed lunch, but you came in time for dessert." Grandma Maria, a short woman, a little on the plump side, with salt-and-pepper hair and kind blue eyes, welcomed him while she carried a pie plate to the table.

Matthew got up and took a peek. "Mmm. Apple pie with custard. My favorite." His heart warmed whenever he was around his grandparents, a welcome feeling after the turbulence with his father.

They sat down at the table while Maria cut slices of pie, topped them with warm vanilla sauce, and handed the plates around. An alluring scent of vanilla tickled Matthew's nose. He took a bite and chewed slowly. He was still thinking about his father and the disagreements they'd had lately.

"You seem to be upset about something." His grandfather, who sat across from him, looked at him with quizzical but warm eyes. "What's bugging you?"

As usual, his grandfather was very perceptive. Matthew put his spoon down and pushed the plate away. "Sometimes I wish I could have a small estate like yours," he said to Sofia and Nicholas. "You did the right thing, Grandpa, when you split the property."

"Yes, I know," Martin said. "I really had no choice. Robert and I had increasingly different ideas about where we wanted to go with the business. Robert was, and still is, ambitious and wanted to expand while I preferred to keep things small and simple. I didn't want to hold him back. So I handed most of the estate over to him and kept my few favorite varietals. It worked out really well." He paused. "Too much for you, the whole thing? Would you prefer a smaller outfit?"

"It's a difficult situation. Don't get me wrong. I love the winery, the estate. Dad did a great job, building an empire. To be honest, I could've done with just a small village, if you know what I mean. But that's not the real problem. I don't really know where I'm going. I mean I'm not even sure of my position. Romero is the manager, and that's cool. He's been a longtime loyal and great employee. Dad loves him. But as far as my place in the business is concerned, I'm more or less just the son of the owner. Dad gives me tons of responsibility but not enough control to actually follow through."

"But you will be the owner one day, you and Nadia," Maria remarked.

"Yes, but you don't think Dad's going to retire any time soon, do you?" Matthew chuckled. "And I don't want him to. I want him to work as long as he can and as long as he wants to. I still have tons to learn. But I have a few ideas for changes, and I don't know how to go about implementing them."

"You mentioned something about the cellar," Nicholas said.

"Yes, as you know we have this grand underground cellar. It was meant to be a place for storing the wine barrels, of course, but initially we thought we would turn part of it into an entertainment venue. That was the original idea, but with Dad gone so much and I not having any real authority, nothing has happened with it."

"You have anything concrete in mind?" his grandfather asked.

"Well, yes, for instance we could set aside an area where people could drink wine, enjoy some food, which we could provide or cater. We could even add live music. I wouldn't want it to be one of those exclusive, snooty outfits that nobody but the rich can afford. It would have to be something for the everyday person. And we could even rent it out for parties. Know what I mean?" Matthew looked at Nicholas.

"That sounds like a great idea. Have you told Dad about it?" his brother asked.

"Many times."

"What did he say?" Sofia asked.

"He says it's great. Go ahead and do it." Matthew rolled his eyes. "That's easily said, but I need a little help. I have no access to the estate money. I couldn't do any renovations and order supplies or hire people without some cash." Matthew winced embarrassed. "I'm sorry. I don't mean to whine."

Martin nodded. "Okay, I can see your problem. May I make a suggestion?"

"Of course."

"Sit down and draw up a plan of the cellar. Try to be as specific as possible. How big do you want the entertainment area to be? Make a diagram. Draw a picture. And then ask around, try to figure out how much it would cost. You want to hire musicians? There are some great local ones. Call them and ask them how much they would charge. Put everything on paper. Make a spreadsheet on the computer. You need to show your father that you are in fact independent, that you not only have ideas, but have a way of making them into reality. I bet you'll get his attention that way."

"You're right. Why didn't I think of that before?"

"Because you're frustrated with your father," Martin said. "I can understand why. He's not an easy man to deal with sometimes. He wants control. So, now, *you* must take control. I bet, once Robert realizes you're not just a dreamer but a doer, he'll begin to listen."

"Grandpa, you are damn smart, you know that?" Matthew laughed. "Thanks. I'm feeling a lot better."

Martin grinned. "Don't forget, he's my son. I know a little how his mind works."

"These are great ideas," Nicholas said. "And if we can help with anything, let us know."

Matthew smiled. "Thanks, guys. I knew I could depend on you. Well, I better get back. Ken wants to discuss some accounting stuff with me."

He got up and kissed his grandmother. "Thanks for the pie, Grandma." As he walked toward the door, his eyes fell on a college catalog. He turned to Sofia.

"By the way, I haven't seen your sister in a while. How's Julietta doing at Cal Poly?"

"Great," Sofia said. "She's wrapping up her finals. She should be home in a couple of weeks. I think she's done really well with her classes."

"Good to hear." Matthew gave everyone a quick good-bye wave and left.

Chapter 2

Julietta Santucci put on lip gloss and combed her shoulder-length auburn hair in front of the mirror in one of the ladies' rooms at California Polytechnic State University.

Cindy, her friend and roommate, stood next to her. "Ah, vacation time. I can't wait."

"I know what you mean. Almost all the finals done. What a relief."

"Are you going somewhere for the summer?" Cindy asked.

"No, I'll be here, well, not here at school but at my sister's place over the holidays. What about you?"

"My parents invited me to go on a trip to Canada with them."

"Oh, that sounds like fun. You'll have a good time."

"Hope so." Cindy shouldered her purse. "Well, gotta go."

"See you at the apartment." Julietta waved as Cindy left the restroom. She picked up her backpack and went to the bookstore, greeting a few fellow students on the way.

After checking out the books for the following term, she walked to the cafeteria. Once again, she marveled at how modern and expansive the university was. She loved it; it was so different from the schools she had attended in her hometown in Italy, where many buildings were old and ornate. Here everything was made of modern materials. As a student of architecture, the construction of buildings had always fascinated her.

Inside the cafeteria, she inhaled the bittersweet scent of coffee and pastry. A fellow student named Adam joined her. Julietta had several classes with him, and she liked him. He was kind, intelligent, and had a good sense of humor. They shared an interest in environment-friendly architecture.

They sat down with their lattes. Julietta looked around the busy cafeteria, listening to the murmuring and occasional laughter of the other students. She stretched with a relieved sigh. "I'm so looking forward to vacation time and working at my sister's vineyards. My first term at Cal Poly is almost over. Thank God."

Adam smiled. "Sounds like you did really well."

"Yes, I'm happy. I was so nervous at first. I had no idea how hard the classes were going to be. They were demanding, but I managed to keep up. With your help. Thanks, Adam."

"Oh, come on, you did very well on your own. Besides, I was happy to have someone help me out at first as well." Adam took a sip of coffee. "By the way, you promised to tell me the reason why you came to live and study here. You dropped some hints and made me very curious."

Julietta chuckled. "Oh, yes, it's quite a story."

"I'm all ears." Adam folded his arms in front of his chest and smiled at her.

Julietta drank some of her latte. At first, she had missed the strong espresso and cappuccino she was familiar with from Italy, but she had acquired a taste for the flavored specialty coffees in California.

"Well, I mentioned that I have a half-sister here," she continued. "Sofia and I have the same father but different mothers."

Adam nodded.

"Okay, my father, or rather our father, was into wines and winemaking here in California and he traveled to Italy a lot, usually to Tuscany. That was before I was born. He also came to Vignaverde to our estate. He and my mother fell in love, and I'm the result of their love." Julietta gave a half-shrug.

"A very beautiful result." Adam's eyes lit up.

"Thanks." Julietta smiled. "The problem was, Henry, my dad, was still married to Sofia's mother. But the marriage was in deep trouble, and then Sofia's mother died of a drug overdose." Julietta looked at him thoughtfully. "My mother later told me that my father felt guilty for having had an affair when his wife was so deeply troubled. Anyway, the relationship between my mother and my father came to an end, and he never told his American family about us, my mother and me. He kept it a secret."

"That sounds cruel," Adam said.

"Well, yes, it wasn't right. But I can understand his situation and although my parents had broken up, they remained friends, and he was a wonderful father to me. He always supported us, and he spent as much time as possible in Vignaverde. I have fond memories of those times. I really miss him." Julietta's voice trembled a little.

"I'm sorry. I didn't mean to badmouth your father. I don't know the situation anyway. What about your sister though? Did she know? About his relationship with your mother and about you?"

Julietta shook her head. "She found out after our father died unexpectedly. He had wanted to come clean. We read that in his journal they found after his death, but he didn't get the chance. It was a terrible shock for Sofia. She came to Vignaverde because she inherited part of our estate, and she wanted to meet me." Julietta looked down at her hands, then faced Adam again.

"I remember so well when I first saw her. I recognized her right away. She looked a lot like me. She was slimmer and taller and had brown hair with blond highlights, but the same facial features and the same eye color."

"Then she must have the same beautiful eyes as you," Adam said. "What an unusual color. Something between purple and blue. Very attractive."

Julietta felt herself blush. "Thanks. We inherited our eyes from our father. Anyway," she continued, "it was a very emotional and turbulent time for all of us, my mother, my uncle and his family, and for me and Sofia, of course. But it all had a good ending. I finally met my sister, we love each other, and Sofia has a great relationship with my family. I love my American family, and I get to study here."

"Wow. What a story. Fascinating. You could write a novel about it." Adam briefly touched Julietta's arm. "I'm happy for you. And I'm happy about the way the story turned out. I'm glad you're here."

Julietta was surprised at his ardent tone. They'd been good friends, but Adam almost sounded like he wanted to get closer to her. He was an interesting man and, yes, very good-looking with his longish, wavy blond hair and the ice-blue eyes. He was tall and trim. She knew he worked out a lot and loved to hike.

Adam cleared his throat. "Any plans for vacation?"

"Well, I'm going to work at my sister and brother-in-law's vineyard. And I'll do a little babysitting for my first nephew. He's due to arrive in June. I'm so excited."

"That sounds great," Adam said. "I'll have to find some kind of work for a while as well and spend some time preparing for next term. I should've looked for a job earlier, but I just didn't have time. It'll be tough to find anything this late. Probably everything is already taken." He paused. "You don't think your sister needs another person helping out at the vineyard, do you?"

"I can ask, but I doubt that Sofia and Nicholas need anybody else, since their part of the estate is fairly small. Of course, I don't know. But Nicholas's father, Robert Segantino, always needs temporary help. His part of the estate is much larger."

"Segantino? Sounds familiar." Adam wrinkled his forehead. "I think my father had a bottle of wine with the Segantino label, and he really liked it."

"Well, I'll check and let you know if anything is available."

"That would be great."

"I'll call your cell or send you a text." Julietta checked her smartphone to make sure she had Adam's number.

"Perfect. Listen, would you like to go out for dinner … pizza or something else?"

Julietta smiled. "Sure, I'd like that."

Later, in the evening, Julietta called Adam to tell him that she had talked to Robert Segantino's accountant, Ken Miller, who, in fact, needed someone to help him with a lot of data entry for a few weeks.

"It wouldn't be working in the vineyards themselves, and it might be somewhat boring office work. Would you be interested?"

"Oh, yes, I don't care how boring it is." Adam laughed. "Besides, I have more experience with computers and figures than with working in the fields."

"Great. Ken said to give him a call to set up an appointment."

"Thanks, Julietta, I really appreciate this."

"No problem, Adam. I'm glad I can help. Ken is an easygoing guy. I think you'll love working with him."

"I'm looking forward to it. And to being near you this summer."

After hanging up, Julietta stepped to the window of her graduate student apartment. It was large, modern, and sunny. She felt lucky to have secured such comfortable lodging, and she was pleased with her roommate, who was a quiet and studious person, not like some of the students she had shared rooms with in Italy, who had been more interested in partying than studying.

She glanced at the tall birch tree in front of the building, its small leaves trembling in the evening breeze. Behind the rolling yellow and green hills, the sun was about to set on the horizon, coloring the sky a light purple. A smile spread across her face. *Adam really is a great guy.*

Chapter 3

"I'll see you again soon." Ken Miller shook Adam's hand. "Having someone help me get rid of this paperwork is going to be a big burden off my back."

"Great, and thanks. I look forward to working with you," Adam said. The two stepped outside. Adam motioned at the stretches of vineyards all around them. "It's such a beautiful place."

Ken nodded. "It is, isn't it? It's a great environment. They also have guided tours around the property and through the winery, if you're interested in that kind of stuff."

"I am. I'd like to find out more. Growing grapes and making wine sounds like a fascinating process. Anyway, see you Monday, and thanks again."

Ken watched him walk down the hill. *Seems like a nice young man.* He checked his watch, then went inside to clean up before leaving for home.

He picked up a couple of personal bills he was getting ready to pay. Perusing his wife's credit card statement, he raised an eyebrow. Five-hundred dollars at Nordstrom? He groaned and stuck the bills into his briefcase. He didn't begrudge Anna some new clothes once in a while, but she had become a real spender. She came from a wealthy family and always had liked beautiful things. He didn't mind as long as they stayed within their budget. He made decent money, but Anna was a stay-at-home mother with expensive tastes. They'd had quite a few arguments about money lately, which had soured their relationship.

He drove the short distance to Atascadero and parked in the driveway of their townhouse. When he opened the door, it was quiet inside. "Anna?"

"In here," his wife called from the bedroom."

He glanced into the kitchen and noticed surprised that it was clean, no signs of dinner preparation. *Was she going out again?*

Anna stepped out of the bedroom. She was dressed in a light-green, expensive-looking two-piece outfit, obviously ready for an evening out.

"Where are you going?" Ken asked with a sinking heart. He had hoped to spend a pleasant evening with his wife.

"I'm going out with Emilia. It's our new bridge evening. I told you days ago." She rolled her eyes. "You never listen."

Ken rubbed his forehead. "Yes, I remember you told me. Sorry, I've had a lot on my mind." He checked his watch. "Where are the kids?"

"They'll be home later. They're having dinner at my parents after their swim practice. Your dinner is in the refrigerator. You just need to heat it up in the microwave."

"All right. Thanks, sweetie." He looked her up and down. "You sure are all gussied up for a bridge evening. New dress?"

Anna smiled. "Yes. You like it?"

"It's lovely ... is this part of the five-hundred-dollar charge from Nordstrom by any chance?" He tried to sound lighthearted about it, but he obviously couldn't fool her.

"Checking my spending again?" Her voice sounded bitter.

"Just wondering. I mean, it's a gorgeous outfit but five-hundred dollars?" He knew he should've let it go.

She glared at him. "I also bought shoes and a purse. You know you're such a cheapskate sometimes. If you made a decent salary—"

"Anna, we've been through this. I *make* a decent salary. We live a very comfortable life. All I'm asking is that you stick to our budget."

"Why don't you ask for a raise?" Anna said. "Jesus, I can't help it when you get taken advantage of by your employer. When was the last time you got a raise?"

"You know exactly when. I can't ask him all the time. He's on a budget, too."

"You mean that rich guy? He's using you."

"No, he's not. He is a great employer. I enjoy my work."

"That's because you have no drive."

"Please, let's not fight. If you want more stuff, get a job yourself."

"And who would take care of the kids?"

"Come on, Michael and Karen are in school a big part of the day. You could get some part-time work, just for pocket money."

"What do you think Daddy would say if he found out that I have to work because my husband is unable to support a small family of four?"

"My God, most women work these days. I could even get you something at the estate. Some office work. We're always short."

"Forget it. Besides, I do work. I volunteer at the women's club."

"Well, yes, but you don't get paid for it. You just have to be a little realistic. I'll work as hard as I can and eventually, I'll get another raise, but for right now, we have to live with what we have."

Anna rolled her eyes. "Whatever." She glanced at her watch. "I need to leave." She still sounded angry.

"Come on, honey, don't be that way. You know I love you, and I want us to be happy, both of us." He followed her to the door. "I'll take care of the money, don't worry. Okay?"

"Okay, need to run. I may come home a little late. Don't wait up for me." She gave him a quick kiss and disappeared.

After Anna left, sadness flooded Ken. How had it come to this? They used to be so happy in the beginning of their relationship. Ken knew that Anna's family had hoped for a better match for their only daughter, someone from their own class and social standing. But Anna had defied them, saying that a loving husband and a close-knit family were more important than all their money and social class. She had resented them for leaving her alone a lot with nannies when she was growing up and was determined not to do that to her children. And she had been a good stay-at-home mother. They lived a modest but decent life. Until … and Ken didn't know exactly when the dissatisfaction had begun. Once the children were in school most of the day, Anna's interests changed. She began to resent the fact that they were always outsiders, the "poor relatives" at the family gatherings and her parents' upscale parties.

Ken stepped into the bedroom, took off his shirt and pants and slipped into a pair of jeans and a T-shirt. He glanced at himself in the mirror. A trim man with only a hint of a forming paunch looked back at him with troubled pale-blue eyes. Quickly brushing through his blond thinning hair, he sighed. He loved Anna and hoped her dissatisfaction was a temporary phase. He'd encouraged her to either get a job or become involved in meaningful work somehow. The result was that she joined the women's volunteer group her mother belonged to. Unfortunately, that wasn't exactly the environment that would make her happier. He suspected her mother's doubts about his qualifications and social standing had begun to take effect in her daughter's mind.

He needed to do something, make more money somehow to prove to her that he wasn't just a lowly accountant but had ambition. Perhaps, he should sign up for the CPA class. That would give him more leverage also with his employer. In fact, Robert had suggested it so he wouldn't need an outside tax preparer anymore. But becoming a CPA would take some time. Would their marriage last that long?

In the living room, he glanced at a photo on the mantelpiece above the fireplace. It showed a younger version of him and his wife as well as their two children as toddlers. He gave a wistful smile. Anna had been and still was a beautiful woman with wavy blond hair and expressive dark eyes. She didn't seem to have aged at all.

They used to be so happy. He needed the relationship to last, for his and Anna's sake and for their children. Perhaps he could come up with something else in the meantime. *Rob a bank, for instance.* His smirk gave way to a sigh.

Chapter 4

Sofia unwrapped another package and held up a tiny denim outfit for a six-month-old baby. "Oh, look how cute." She chuckled as she passed it around for her family and friends to see. "I know I'm going to say that all day."

Her family was giving Sofia a baby shower. Janice, her mother-in-law, Grandma Maria, Julietta, her sister, as well as Juanita and Nora Guerrero, the manager's wife and daughter, were gathered at the grandparents' house, eating cake, drinking lemonade and coffee, and admiring the presents. Baby clothes, toys, gift coupons for diapers and baby food, an empty photo book were spread out on the coffee table. A colorful mobile was hanging over the crib Robert and Janice had bought for them.

"Thank you, guys, this is wonderful," Sofia said and hugged Janice, who was sitting next to her.

When she opened the present Juanita and Nora gave her, she gasped. She unwrapped a beautiful quilted blanket for the crib. It was made of tiny squares of cloth in many different colors, lovingly assembled and stitched together. "This is absolutely gorgeous. Look at these colors."

"Nora made it," Juanita said.

"What? You made that by yourself? This is amazing." Sofia looked at the girl.

"Well, my mother helped a little," Nora said. She was a slim, pretty fifteen-year-old with long black hair and large dark eyes. She was suffering from multiple sclerosis and was confined to a wheelchair. As Sofia knew, Nora was Juanita and Romero's only child and both a blessing and a heartbreak for her parents.

"This is so beautiful. Thank you." Sofia got up and embraced Nora, who gave a quick embarrassed smile.

The door opened halfway and Nicholas peeked into the room. "Are men allowed in this shindig?"

"Come on in," Maria called, laughing. "We make exceptions for husbands … and grandfathers and, of course, managers," she added as Martin and Romero followed Nicholas inside.

Nicholas and Martin took a quick look at the gifts, then walked over to the table with the sweets and coffee. Romero stood next to his wife and daughter. He was a slim man in his late forties of medium height with black hair streaked with gray and dark eyes that always looked a little troubled.

"Romero, I absolutely love this." Sofia held up the quilt. "It's so beautiful."

Romero smiled and for once his sad eyes lit up. "Nora made it."

"I know. It's amazing." Sofia handed the quilt to Maria and Janice, who admired it. "Perfect stitching," Maria said to Nora. "You really did a great job. I used to be part of a quilting group with a few other women, and your work is as good as any we did."

Romero touched Nora's shoulder. She grabbed his hand and held it in hers. Sofia sensed the close bond between father and daughter. She knew that Romero and Juanita worried a lot about Nora, of what would become of her if anything ever happened to them, who would look after her, should she survive them both.

"Romero, come on over here and have some coffee and sweets," Martin said.

"Help yourselves." Sofia chuckled. "I know that's what you and Nicholas really came for, not the baby stuff."

Nicholas shoved his sun-bleached hair away from his face. "Not true. Well, perhaps a little. You know how much we love Grandma's pastry." His eyes lit up with a mischievous glint as he bit into a tart. He gobbled half of it before stopping to sip his coffee, and then finished it off as he gazed around the room. "Ah, toys," he said. He set down his cup and walked to the gift table. He picked up a carved wooden train car. "Why, look at this."

"Isn't it cute?" Sofia said. "Uncle Angelo made it."

"Wow," Nicholas said. "I didn't know he was artistic like this."

Angelo, who was Martin's younger brother and great-uncle to Sofia and Nicholas, lived about twenty-five miles south, in San Luis Obispo. He and his wife, Miriam, were out of town and hence missed the baby shower.

"Are you finished with the racking?" Sofia asked Nicholas, referring to a process at the winery, when the fermenting wine was separated from the leftover solids.

"Yep, with Romero, Grandpa, and Matt helping, it went fast. By the way, Matt will be here in a few minutes," Nicholas said.

"Where's Robert these days?" Sofia asked. "I haven't seen him around in a while."

"On one of his many trips," Janice said. "He's in Spain promoting one of our wines once again."

"Do you mind that he's gone so much?" Sofia asked.

Janice shrugged. "I got used to it. In the beginning, I went with him quite often, but lately, I've grown tired of the constant trips. I agree with Matt. He takes these wine contests too far. How many more awards can he put up in his office? I understand him visiting his clients personally. That's important to maintain relationships. The rest is superfluous, I think."

"Yes, he should focus more on the estate itself," Martin said. "But he'll realize it one day. He's stubborn. It has to be his idea to make changes."

"Exactly." Janice nodded. "That's why I stopped mentioning it. He'll come around."

Grandma Maria turned to Julietta who sat next to her. "Have some more pie and coffee."

"Thanks. No more pie for me. I have to watch my weight. Too much junk food at the college." Julietta patted her hips.

"When are you coming home for the summer?" Maria asked.

"Soon. The spring term ends at the beginning of June. I'm really looking forward to working in a vineyard again." Julietta smiled. "And helping to take care of little Henry, of course." She patted Sofia's bulging belly.

"I'll be very grateful for the help," Sofia said. "Ouch, he kicked." She put her hand on her belly. "He must agree."

"I heard that a fellow student is coming to work during the summer," Nicholas said to Julietta.

"Yes, I saw him in Ken's office the other day." Sofia turned to Julietta. "A very attractive young man."

"Oh, yes. Adam is very nice."

Sofia noticed her sister blushing. "Hmm. Sounds like romance could be in the air."

"Oh, I don't know," Julietta said. "We went out a few times, but we're just friends."

At that moment, the door opened and Matthew stepped inside. He removed his baseball cap and wiped the sweat from his forehead. "Gee, it's hot out there." He kissed Sofia and put a package into her lap, then walked over to the table with the sweets. "Now, what do we have here?"

"Help yourself, honey." Maria got up, poured him a cup of coffee, and pushed the plate of strawberry tarts toward him.

"Thanks, Grandma. You don't need to tell me twice." Matthew took a bite of the pastry. "Although I should really watch my calories. The scale gave me a shock the other day." He laid a hand on his stomach.

Matthew didn't resemble his older brother at all, at least not in looks. While Nicholas took after their mother—he was tall, slim and had light-blond hair and brown eyes—Matthew had inherited their father's Italian features. Like Robert, he was of medium height, somewhat stocky and had dark, curly hair and dark, almost black, eyes.

"Oh, come on, Matt," Sofia said, as Matthew sat next to her. "It's all muscles."

"Thank you, my dear, but I know better."

"Matt, these are so cute. Thanks." Sofia held up two tiny outfits, one with the Paso Robles logo and one with the picture of a race car on it."

Janice pointed at the outfit with the picture of a car on it. "You think your future nephew will be a car fanatic like you are?"

Matthew shrugged and smiled. "I can always hope. Once I get too old to drive, he can chauffeur me around."

"How is your new baby?" Nicholas asked.

"You mean the one with the four wheels?" Matthew winked at him. "Perfect. I just gave it a thorough cleaning and polishing." He hesitated. "Although I still feel a little guilty for splurging. The conservative thing would've been to pay off my student loan first. But it was such a great deal. I was afraid if I waited, it would be gone."

"Well, Matt, you deserve a little luxury once in a while, too. You work very hard," Janice said.

"Thanks, Mom."

"What year is it again?" Martin asked.

"A ninety-one Porsche convertible," Matthew said. "It's really a classic car."

"Great." Martin smiled. "You have to give me a ride sometime."

"I will, Grandpa. But you can drive it yourself anytime you want."

"Ah, no. I prefer to be driven."

"All right. What about this coming Saturday?" Matthew asked.

Martin gave a thumbs up. "It's a deal."

"By the way, when is Dad coming back from Spain?" Matthew turned to Janice.

"The last weekend in June," Janice said. "I'll pick him up at the airport."

"Good. Romero and I need to talk to him. I really hope he'll be around for a while. We decided to physically tie him to his chair in the office, so he can't leave. Right, Romero?"

Romero nodded and a quick smile flashed across his face.

Matthew looked at him thoughtfully. "Romero, I don't know how you do it. You seem to always get along with Dad. He sometimes yells at you and you just shrug it off. I wish I had your even temper."

Romero gave another quick smile. "I don't take his outbursts personally. He is a little impatient sometimes, but he is a good man. He has a good heart. My family and I owe him a lot."

"How long have you worked for us, Romero?" Janice frowned. "About twelve or thirteen years, right?"

Romero nodded. "It will be sixteen years this fall." He cleared his throat and continued in his mild-mannered voice. "We'd just had a baby." He smiled at Nora. "I lost my job as a sommelier at a restaurant—one of Segantino Winery's customers. The owner of the restaurant moved to the East Coast and the outfit closed. I knew about wine, but I had no experience working for an actual winery. Robert hired me on the spot, and here we are."

"Well, you learned very quickly," Janice said. "Robert is very grateful to have you."

"Thank you," Romero whispered. His eyes had the usual somber expression again.

Chapter 5

"Congratulations!" Julietta and Sofia greeted Robert as he walked into the tasting room after his return from Europe, where the Syrah he submitted at the contest in Spain had won another award.

"Thanks, guys." Robert gave them the thumbs up. "This isn't just a win for me, but for the estate. So, congratulations to all of you as well." He walked over to Sofia who held the newest member of the Segantino family in her arms. Little Henry had been born three weeks before while Robert was in Spain. Sofia handed him the baby. He held his grandchild in his arms and kissed the little boy's head. "You, too, won an award. You're our next generation." Henry opened his blue eyes, then closed them again, opened his mouth wide and yawned. Robert smiled and cradled the baby a while before handing him back to Sofia.

Julietta noticed that Robert was in a good mood. He had a big smile on his face, and his usually dark piercing eyes looked warm and mild. He glanced at Julietta and Adam who stood next to Sofia.

"Uncle Robert, this is Adam. He's a friend of mine from college, and he works with Ken in Accounting for the summer. He hasn't had a chance to really look around yet. I'm going to give him a tour. He said his family knows our wine and they love it. He wants to see how it's made."

"Welcome." Robert shook Adam's hand. "Ken told me you were a great help."

"Thanks," Adam said. "There is quite a backlog of data to be entered, but we're catching up. Thank you for letting me work here. What an interesting place. I'm learning a lot."

"You're welcome. So you're a student at Cal Poly as well?"

"Yes. Julietta and I are in the same program."

"Adam is a year ahead of me. He helps me out a lot."

"Wonderful," Robert said. "Enjoy the tour. Come back and taste some wine. You're old enough to drink, right?"

"Yes, I'm twenty-two."

"Great. See you later then."

"Are you even allowed in the tasting room, since you're not twenty-one yet?" Adam asked Julietta as they began walking through the estate.

"Yes, that's fine. They don't just sell wine, they have things such as marmalade, olives, and other delicacies that underage people can buy. I'm just not allowed to taste wine. Robert could really get into trouble with the law if I was caught. At home, in my sister's home, I mean, I can drink wine. I'm not much into alcohol. I didn't even like wine when I lived on our estate in Tuscany. But I'm starting to develop a taste for it."

"Yeah, I'm not a big drinker myself, but I do like an occasional glass of red wine," Adam said.

They walked through the estate, along some of the vineyards, and Julietta showed him the area with the fermentation tanks, the crusher, the wine press, and the large underground cellar.

Adam crinkled his nose and inhaled. "Interesting smell. I like it."

"Yes, I know." Julietta inhaled deeply. "I love it, too. It's the French oak barrels ... or a combination of aging wine and oak." She chuckled. "Reminds me of home."

"This is really great." Adam was surveying the rows of barrels in the cellar. He pointed at an area with tables, chairs, and wooden benches. "What's this for?"

"They're planning to use it for entertainment," Julietta explained. "They'll have food and wine and rent it out for parties. Matthew, Nicholas's brother, who works here as well, is in charge of developing the cellar. He also plans to invite musicians for live music."

"Splendid idea. I wouldn't mind coming here for entertainment. This is quite unique," Adam said. "I have a friend who plays saxophone in a jazz band. He may be interested."

"You should definitely tell Matthew about it. He's looking for local bands."

After a stroll through the vineyards and the cellar, they walked back to the tasting room. A few customers were there, talking to Robert and sipping wine or browsing the gift items and accessories. Sofia and Janice were helping out.

"Where is Henry?" Julietta asked, looking around the room.

Sofia motioned toward the back, where the baby was fast asleep in his buggy. "He's conked out, he woke up a few times at night and he's been up since the crack of dawn." Sofia suppressed a yawn. "But once we got here, he fell asleep, so I didn't want to disturb him. I'm going to take him over to Grandma's in a while. I need to feed him."

"I bet it's the wine fumes." Robert chuckled. "Calms him down."

"Nonsense." Janice laughed. "He's just been busy tiring out his mom and dad. Since he accomplished that, now he can go to sleep. Our kids did that all the time."

"Did you like your tour?" Robert asked Adam.

"Yes, it's great. I really loved the underground cellar. I heard you're planning to have entertainment for guests there."

"Yeah, Matt, my son, is in charge of organizing it." Robert grabbed a bottle of red wine. "You said you tasted some of our wine. What kind was it?"

Adam scrunched his forehead. "Oh, I think it was a Cabernet."

"Where did you get it?"

"Actually, my uncle got it for us. I don't know where he got it. My parents and I loved it a lot and my father said he wanted to order some."

"Since you know our Cab, you may want to try something else. Here is a list of what's available for tasting."

"Thanks." Adam looked at the list. "Oh, you have Sangiovese? I'd love to try some."

"Okay. Do you have identification? Not that I don't trust you, but by law I'm obligated to check."

"No problem." Adam pulled out his wallet and searched for his driver's license while Robert poured him a small glass of Sangiovese.

"This is actually from the cellar of Sofia and Nicholas Segantino." He motioned at Sofia. "My daughter-in-law. Nicholas is my other son."

"Okay, so the whole family is in the wine business?" Adam remarked.

"Yes, more or less."

Adam handed him his driver's license.

"Thanks." Robert glanced at it and nodded, then before giving it back, he looked at it again. "Your last name is Winter?"

"Yes," Adam said. "Why?"

Robert narrowed his eyes. "Any connection to George Winter?"

Adam nodded. "Yeah, he's my uncle. Actually it's because of him that I know your wine. He brought us a bottle once."

Julietta looked at Robert who kept staring at Adam's driver's license. He finally handed it back to him but seemed puzzled, almost shocked. He gave Adam a serious and measured look. "He worked for the government, right? I met him a couple of times."

"That's right. He used to work for San Luis Obispo City Hall, but that was a while ago." Adam shrugged. "We're not real close. My dad and he are kind of estranged."

Robert continued to look at him bewildered. "Do you know where he got our wine? We usually only sell to restaurants and stores, or to individuals in our wine club. And I'm sure he's not in the club."

"No idea, sorry." Adam shrugged. "It was a family celebration, my father's birthday, and Uncle George came by with a bottle of Segantino wine. I assume he bought it at a store."

Julietta was surprised at Robert's demeanor. He seemed preoccupied.

"Well, whatever. Want to try something else?" After pouring Adam another glass of wine, he joined Janice who was talking to a client.

Julietta noticed though that he kept glancing at Adam and her. She wondered what bothered him. Adam was such a pleasant guy, but Robert stared at them with an almost hostile look. The warmth in his eyes had given way to a sharp, penetrating gaze, which made Julietta feel uncomfortable.

"Let's go outside," she said to Adam. "It's getting too crowded in here."

He looked at her puzzled, then finished his glass and put it on the counter. "Yeah, I guess I should be getting back to work anyway."

Outside, Julietta took a deep breath.

"You're okay?" Adam asked.

"Oh, yes," she lied. "I'm fine. I just remembered I have to do some laundry. Running out of clean clothes."

Adam gave her a quick hug." Thank you for showing me around. That was fascinating."

"I'm glad you liked it," Julietta said. "See you tomorrow, then." She watched as Adam climbed the short path to the office, then turned to gaze at the fields of grapes and the meadows, where the shadows of the oak trees had lengthened in the late afternoon sun. She shook her head, trying to dispel the memory of Robert's strange behavior. *It's probably nothing. Uncle Robert can be moody sometimes.*

Chapter 6

"Why would George Winter buy our wine?" Robert said. "There is no love lost between us. After all, I was in part responsible for him getting fired from his job and ending up in prison." He and Janice were having dinner. Robert finished the last piece of vegetable quiche and put his fork down. He gazed out the window where the sun was getting ready to disappear behind the hills.

It had been a hot day, but in the evening a blistering wind had begun to blow, shaking the trees and hurtling waves of dust across the dried-out fields. As much as Robert liked the dry weather, which helped ripen the grapes, the often-turbulent Santa Ana winds made him feel anxious and gave him headaches. He massaged his temples with his fingers.

The incident three years ago was still fresh in his mind. It was during the height of the drought in California, which led to some acrimonious exchanges between farmers, winemakers, and the tourist industry, each side blaming the other for wasting water. It also resulted in certain government restrictions on the use of water, one of them being a moratorium on new irrigation systems. It was just at the time when Robert decided to replace his old system with a new one that used less water, therefore adding to the conservation effort. His application, however, was rejected, because no new permits were granted, not even for systems that were more efficient and less wasteful.

According to Robert and his fellow vintners and winemakers, that was the kind of meaningless intrusion of a government that didn't really understand the situation. He accepted the decision but then found out by accident that one of the other winemakers had received a permit. He was shocked and together with a couple of his friends he hired an investigator to look into possible unlawful governmental procedures. As it turned out, George Winter was the official who had accepted bribes in exchange for permits. He was fired from his job and spent some time in prison. Robert never heard another word about Winter until the day Adam showed him his driver's license. He couldn't shake the feeling that this wasn't a coincidence.

Janice interrupted his musing. "Did Winter know it was you who turned him in?"

"Oh, he knew all right," Robert said.

"Perhaps, someone gave him the wine as a present," Janice suggested. "Since he may not have wanted to drink it himself, he gave it to Adam's father. I don't know. Perhaps just a coincidence."

"I guess so. Still, it's odd." Robert rubbed his forehead. "I didn't realize Adam was related to him. Not sure I would've hired him, had I known."

"Well, you don't think Adam is a bad person just because his uncle is a crook. Besides, he told you that they weren't close," Janice said.

"I know, but still, having the nephew of one of my enemies on the estate is not very reassuring."

"I think you might be making too much of this. George may not like you very much, but you weren't the only one who got him into trouble with the law. Others testified as well. Besides, Adam seems to be a very nice person. And as Ken told you, he does good work."

"Yeah, I know." Robert shrugged. "You're probably right. I may be a little too paranoid." He got up and helped his wife clear the table.

In the kitchen, Janice pressed the button on their espresso machine and put two small cups under the spout. She grabbed a bottle of grappa and gave Robert a questioning look. He nodded.

"Yeah, I'll have a little bit."

Janice topped their espresso off with a shot of grappa and carried the two cups into the dining room.

"By the way, did you talk to Matt about his plans for the cellar and the estate?" Janice asked.

Robert nodded. "Yes, we had a talk."

"And?" Janice asked. "What did you decide?"

Robert who had been stirring his espresso, looked up. He took a sip and smacked his lips. The grappa added a pleasant spark to the slightly bitter coffee." I'll give him access to one of the accounts, so he can go ahead with his plan for the cellar."

"Good. Make sure you do it, though," Janice said. "Matt seems a little frustrated, not having much authority."

Robert took another sip, then set his cup down. "Yeah, well, Matt is a good guy but a dreamer. He needs to toughen up and show some initiative. Authority needs to be earned."

"What are you talking about?" Janice stared at him. "Matt has been working hard for you and he has good ideas. But how can he put them into practice if he doesn't have the resources? And you're gone all the time."

"Oh, stop that old song." Robert felt a spike of irritation. "I hear that enough from Matt. He's an adult. He can make decisions. I'll sign anything that sounds reasonable to me. Problem is, Matt is too soft. Yes, he works hard, but he doesn't have to do all the small stuff he always does. He needs to learn to delegate. Once he runs the winery, he won't be able to do everything himself." Robert got up. "Sometimes I wonder if he is the right person to take over. I would've preferred Nicholas. He is older and more experienced, but he copped out."

"For God's sake, Robert, how can you say that? One of the reasons Nicholas turned down your offer to manage the place is that it's too big for him. He is more like your father in that respect. He prefers to be directly involved in the work. Just because he has other ideas doesn't mean he's a cop-out. And Matt enjoys the actual work at the winery as well. That's why he does it, not because he doesn't know how to delegate."

"I didn't say Nick was a cop-out." Robert waved his hand in a dismissive gesture. "He turned down the inheritance, which I still regret sometimes. But it was his decision, so I accept it. But Matt agreed to take over once I retire, so he has to learn the ropes. And part of it is how to run a large estate like ours."

"Don't be such a tyrant," Janice said. "You can't expect your children to follow exactly in your footsteps. They have to grow and develop at their own pace."

"All right, all right. I get the point. I don't feel like arguing." Robert picked up his empty cup and carried it into the kitchen. He stepped outside onto the patio and let his eyes wander over the fields and the hills of his vast estate. The turbulent winds had died down, giving way to a gentler breeze.

The air now felt clear and invigorating. The sun had set and the sky at the horizon was a deep purple. Robert's irritation faded, and his heart swelled with joy at the thought of how his estate and winemaking business had developed. He knew his wife meant well. Perhaps she was right, and he should ease off a little and not pressure Matt too much. He just wanted him to be strong and capable enough to continue the Segantino heritage his father had begun and he wanted to continue to develop. It was a family business, and family was important to him. *Must be our Italian roots.*

Chapter 7

George, Norman, and their friends were playing poker in George's apartment in San Luis Obispo. George was in a bad mood; he kept losing. It seemed that Norman was the only one who won regularly. Two of their buddies had already dropped out, complaining there was too much of a difference between the players' skills, and they were tired of losing all the time.

On top of it, George had a headache. He attributed it to the strange weather. It had been a stifling hot day, and now a fierce dry wind was howling. The light in the apartment flickered several times, making it hard for him to concentrate on the game. The frowns on the faces of the players and a resigned groan of one of his partners told him he was not the only one getting frustrated.

At the end of the game, Norman got up. "Perhaps we should stop playing for money. I don't think this is fun for you."

"Well, you're just too good for us," one of the guys said. "You're a professional."

Norman raised an eyebrow. "I used to play professionally, whatever that means. If you want to learn how to gamble, I could teach you, but I don't think that's what you want. So, let's just play cards without money. What do you think?" He glanced at George, who shrugged.

"Fine with me. I'm going bankrupt otherwise," George grumbled. "Okay, next time, just a friendly card game."

The other men nodded, got up, and left one after the other. Norman was getting ready to leave as well, but George held him by the arm. "Let's have another beer."

Norman hesitated, checked his watch, and sat back down. "All right, but only one more."

George went into his bedroom where he kept a safe. He keyed in the code, opened the safe, took out two thousand dollars, and stuffed the bills into an envelope. In the kitchen, he pulled two bottles of Corona, Norman's favorite beer, out of the refrigerator. He put the bottles on the table in the living room, opened them, and pushed one toward Norman.

Norman took a sip, then glanced at his watch again.

"You're in a hurry? Have a hot date tonight?" He grinned. Norman didn't say anything. After weeks of playing and drinking together, this strange man was still an enigma to George. Whereas the other friends hollered and swore or laughed during the game, Norman was always polite, quiet, and focused. This mysterious man was no dummy.

George cleared his throat and shoved the envelope with the money across the table toward Norman.

Norman picked it up. "What's this?"

"Open it," George encouraged him.

Norman opened the envelope and dumped a bunch of one-hundred-dollar bills on the table. He glared at George.

"I've been watching you carefully," George said. "I know I'm a lousy player, but you're excellent. I want you to take this money and play at a casino, you know, the real thing. If you win, we'll split the winnings."

Norman looked at George stunned. He put the money back into the envelope and pushed it across the table. "I can't do that. I don't gamble at casinos anymore."

"Come on, dude. This is free money. If you win, that's great. If you lose, it won't break my bank. This is extra money

I made with a successful business deal." He pushed the envelope toward Norman again.

George watched carefully as different emotions flashed across Norman's face—hesitation, desire, guilt. It was the first time in his encounter with this strange man that he saw weakness, and George rejoiced.

Norman kept staring at the envelope for a long time. In the end he picked it up. "I shouldn't do this," he mumbled, then in louder voice, "okay, but only this one time."

George finally had him. He was all too familiar with addiction. "Have fun." He grinned.

Outside, on his way to the car, Norman rubbed the envelope in his pocket. Images of past events at the casinos many years before flashed before his eyes. Tables covered in red and green felt, cards, and chips in casinos in Las Vegas. The wheel of fortune, muffled outbursts of elation or despair, the voice of the croupiers crying *"Faites vos jeux,"* that time in Monte Carlo. He had been young and adventurous with a knack for gambling. His naturally calm, cool, and observant temperament and an almost photographic memory were ideal for this venture.

Together with a friend he had traveled the world in search of excitement and money and temporary lovers in different cities, without any serious relationships to tie him down. It was the high life. Most of all, however, it was the thrill of winning and, even though that high was only temporary, followed by the low of losing, the highs became more and more addictive. That went on for a few years—until the day tragedy struck.

His close friend and gambling buddy began to lose and lose big. One day, he disappeared without a word. His body was found at the bottom of an abyss on a beach in Monte

Carlo. His death was ruled a suicide. Shocked, sad, and full of questions, Norman stopped gambling. Could he have done more to help his friend cover his losses? He offered him money, but his friend was a proud man and didn't want any so-called handouts.

After burying his friend in France, Norman returned to California, trying to decide what to do with the rest of his life. Gambling and the lifestyle associated with it lost its luster, not just because of the tragedy of his friend's death, but for another reason. He fell in love, deeply, for the first time in his life, and decided to settle down. Marriage and the birth of a child followed and his craving for excitement gave way to a sense of belonging, which he cherished. The temptation of gambling was still there, but he'd managed to beat the craving—until the day he met George Winter.

Was he willing to endanger his quiet and secure life by giving in to the allure of excitement? But excitement was only part of the reason he considered the tempting offer from George. Although he made a decent salary, unexpected expenses weighed him down. One win at the casino and he could pay everything off. And if he lost, it wasn't even his money.

He glanced at the trees in the yard next to his parked car. They were bending in the gusty wind. It smelled of dry grass and exhaust from the city streets.

He pushed the warning voices to the back of his mind. "Only once," he told himself as he rubbed the envelope in his pocket again.

Chapter 8

Sofia passed the entrance to the underground cellar on her way to Robert's winery. She took a quick peek inside and smiled as she admired the rows of French oak barrels. When she stepped into the tasting room, she heard Matthew's voice down the hall where the offices were.

He sounded irritated. Thinking that Matthew and Robert were arguing, Sofia stopped, not wanting to intrude. After a few seconds, she realized it was only Matthew she heard, apparently talking on the phone. She heard him mention Nicholas's name.

There was a moment of silence. Then Matthew spoke again. "Sometimes I feel he'd rather have Nick run the show. He never says it outright, but I know he's still disappointed Nick turned him down. I mean, let's face it, I was second choice."

Silence again.

"No, I'm not blowing it out of proportion ... yeah, I know, it's not Nick's fault. Once you're through with your studies and come home, things may improve. There'll be the two of us; we'll have more leverage, more power against his stubbornness." A short laugh followed and Sofia realized that Matthew was talking to his sister Nadia.

"Anyway, he finally gave me access to one of the estate accounts, so I can start putting my plans for the cellar into action. But I still feel he resents it. As if he thought I was trying to enrich myself. I mean, it's for the estate for God's sake."

Sofia tiptoed around the corner and left. She felt guilty for having overheard the talk. She knew things had been tense between Robert and Matthew, but she hadn't realized the ambivalent feelings Matthew seemed to have vis-à-vis his older brother.

Later that evening, Sofia told Nicholas about the conversation she overheard. "I felt kind of bad for eavesdropping, but by the time I realized what he was talking about, I didn't want him to know I heard it."

"Well, it's no secret that Dad and Matt don't always see eye to eye and that Matt is frustrated. Besides, he doesn't have a lot of self-confidence." Nicholas was carrying little Henry around, trying to burp him. Sofia had just finished feeding him.

"Didn't you invite him for dinner tonight?" he asked.

"Yes, I better check on the food. Can you put Henry down for the night?"

"No problem. Come on little beggar. We'll get your diaper changed, and then it's bed time." Henry gurgled and spit. "Hey, no backtalk." Nicholas kissed Henry's head and wiped his mouth before carrying him into the nursery.

Sofia was in the kitchen, checking on the chicken roasting in the oven, when she heard a knock on the door. "Come on in," she called.

"You're a trusting soul," Matthew said as he stepped inside. "What if I'd been a burglar?"

"I'm psychic." Sofia laughed. "I sensed it was you."

Matthew put a bottle of wine on the kitchen counter and kissed her cheek. "Smells good here. Where's the rest of the family?"

"Nicholas is putting Henry to bed. They're in the nursery." Sofia took a plate of vegetables out of the refrigerator and got ready to stir-fry them.

"Have to see that." Matthew left the kitchen. Soon, Sofia heard the two men murmuring in the nursery. She poured the vegetables into the wok and stirred them until they were done. Nicholas came into the kitchen and pulled the chicken out of the oven. He put it on the platter Sofia had set aside.

As usual when he was invited, Matthew dug in and raved about Sofia's cooking. He was a grateful guest, always had a good appetite, and enjoyed not having to cook for himself. While drinking espresso and enjoying a scoop of ice cream for dessert, Nicholas asked Matthew how work was going. Sofia could see the change of mood on Matthew's face. The line between his eyebrows deepened.

"Sometimes, I feel like throwing the whole damn thing in his face."

"Whoa. Doesn't sound good," Nicholas said.

"More coffee?" Sofia asked as she gathered the empty dessert bowls.

"Not for me. Thanks." Matthew gave a quick smile, then his face darkened again.

"Yes, but I'll get it," Nicholas said.

"I'll get it," Sofia said quickly. "You two talk." She was glad to escape the now tense atmosphere. From the kitchen, she could hear them speaking.

"So, what's going on?" Nicholas asked.

"It's always the same and I hate to sound like a broken record. I hardly ever get the feeling he appreciates me or my work. I feel I'm constantly being compared to you, and I come away lacking."

"What makes you think so? Did he say anything?"

"No, not directly, but I can read between the lines," Matthew said.

"I think you interpret something from Dad's behavior that isn't there. Believe me, if I was in your place, he'd treat me the same way. You know how he is. He's a good man, but he can be a real self-centered control freak as well. Don't let him get to you."

"Easier said than done. I have to work with him."

"Yes, I understand," Nicholas said. "It's a lot of responsibility and can be a hassle sometimes."

Sofia heard a loud sigh. "It's not the responsibility that's the problem," Matthew said. "But I also want to be able to make decisions on my own once in a while, to be able to contribute to the estate. He finally, after all this time, gave me access to one of the estate accounts. But I feel he's afraid I'm going to rob him blind, as if I wanted to use it for myself."

"Are you sure you're not reading more into this than is really there? Dad has always been frugal. Remember how he was when we were kids? When we wanted extra money above our allowance, we always had to earn it. He felt it would harm us if we grew up like many of the rich kids who had everything they wanted without working for it. I think he was right."

"Agreed," Matthew said. "But I'm not a kid anymore. All I want is to feel appreciated and respected."

"And you don't think Dad respects you?"

"I don't know." Matthew sounded dejected.

"Matt, you are good at what you do. And he knows it. But he runs a big outfit that means a lot to him, and that's why he can be too demanding at times. I don't think it's personal. As I said, he'd treat me the same way if I was in your place."

"Perhaps you're right." Matthew didn't sound convinced.

There was silence for a while. Then Nicholas's voice. "What about Grandpa's suggestion that you document your plan for the cellar and the winery? Did you do it?"

"I started, but then other things interfered. But I'll get it done."

"Okay. And I told you before, if you need help, let me know."

"Thanks. But this I'll have to do on my own. Besides, if you help, you'll get all the credit again." Matthew's voice sounded bitter.

"Matt, you're being ridiculous. Why are you angry at *me*? This sounds like outright jealousy. That's not fair."

"I'm sorry. I'm being an ass," Matthew said. "No, it's not fair and yes, I'll ask you if I need help. I just need to bolster my tarnished self-confidence."

"Matt, Dad asked me to take over the business because I'm the oldest, and he knew I wanted to continue working with wine, not because he doesn't appreciate you. He was more than grateful that you and Nadia agreed to take over. He wants to keep the winery in the family."

"Yeah, I know. I just sometimes feel he still regrets that you turned him down."

"If that's true, it's not because he doubts you, but because his pride was hurt. I mean who would turn down such a generous offer from one of the most important vintners and winemakers in the area? And yet his son does it and settles for a small outfit like Grandpa's."

"I guess you have a point," Matthew admitted.

Sofia, who felt that the tension had lessened, came back into the living room. "Is everything okay in here? You two aren't going to kill each other?"

Both men smiled at her as she put Nicholas's espresso on the table.

"No," Matthew said. "Just our usual brotherly jousting."

"You know what your problem is, Matt?" Nicholas put his hand on Matthew's shoulder. "You and Dad are both hotheads. You have the Italian fire in you. No wonder you fight all the time. You're two peas in a pod."

"Don't say that." Matthew looked furious, then his face softened and he laughed. "Oh, well, you may be right."

A few hours later, Matthew left, his mood visibly improved. Sofia and Nicholas had accompanied him outside where they said their good-byes. It had cooled off, and now the two were sitting on the patio, admiring the purple-blue horizon still lit up somewhat by the sun that had set hours ago. Sofia took a deep breath, inhaling the scent of sage.

"It's so beautiful here." She put her arm around Nicholas's shoulder.

"I know," he said. "We're very lucky to live here." He took her hand and kissed it.

Sofia held on to his hand. "I just hope Matt and your father can find a way to have a better relationship. They seem to argue all the time."

"I know what you mean. Problem is, in many ways, they're similar. They're both short-tempered, hotheaded, and impatient. On top of it, Dad is controlling, and Matt has to learn to stand up to him without blowing up. Very difficult."

Sofia smiled. "I'm so glad, we have our own outfit. It's smaller, easier, and I love working with Grandpa."

"Oh, yes. Thank God I made the decision not to take over Dad's estate. It wasn't easy. I know he was disappointed, probably still is. Matt is right about that. But I also believe Matt will enjoy managing the estate once Dad gives him more authority and lets him do his own thing. He has good ideas. He just needs to be a little more organized and confident."

They remained seated for a while, enjoying the peaceful evening. A light breeze teased the Azalea bush next to the patio, making the leaves tremble lightly. Sofia inhaled the spicy-sweet fragrance of the pink and purple blooms. The screeching of a night bird interrupted the quiet.

"Where's Julietta tonight?" Nicholas asked.

"She's out with a friend of hers," Sofia said.

"She adjusted fast to the California lifestyle." Nicholas chortled. "Going out, partying. But she's a serious student, too."

Sofia nodded. "She sure is." After a while, she got up and went to check on Henry, who was sleeping peacefully. When she came back outside, she stood next to Nicholas who was gazing at the fields in front of their home. He put his arm around her and pulled her close.

"Is Henry the Second sleeping?" Nicholas sometimes called him that, since they had named their son after Sofia's father.

"Like an angel," Sofia said and hugged him, craving the warmth of his body.

"Does that mean, we'll have some time to ourselves?" Nicholas kissed her gently, the scent of espresso on his breath. She grasped his head, pulling him closer, kissing him fervently. By the time they came up for breath, Sofia's body was on fire.

"Let's take this inside," Nicholas said, his voice smoky.

Chapter 9

Julietta stood in the shade of an oak tree next to Sofia and Nicholas's home, fanning herself with her sun hat. She was gazing at the horizon for possible clouds and the promise of some relief from the heat. There was nothing. The sky was a dark blue on this Saturday in July.

Adam walked up to her. "Want to take a drive to the coast? It's bound to be cooler there."

"Gee, that sounds inviting," she said. "I haven't been to the coast in ages. Too much work around here."

"Have you ever been to Cambria?" Adam asked.

"Just once for dinner with Sofia and Nicholas. I'd love to explore the California coastline more."

"It would be great to drive to Big Sur. It's an amazing place, but I think the road is closed once again because of a landslide," Adam said. "But we could check out the elephant seals and drive at least to Ragged Point and have lunch or dinner there."

"Oh, yes, that sounds wonderful. I've seen pictures of the elephant seal sanctuary but have never seen it in person."

Adam put his arm around her. "Well, let me be your travel guide for the day. What do you say?"

"Perfect. You're hired." Julietta inhaled his lemon-scented shaving lotion. "Let me just tell my sister." They walked up to the house, and Julietta went inside. Sofia was putting little Henry down for his mid-morning nap.

"Adam and I are driving to the coast. He wants to show me the elephant seals," Julietta said.

Sofia winked at her. "Sounds great."

"What are you winking at me for?"

"Well, you know." Sofia wiggled her eyebrow. "I understand. He's very nice and handsome to boot."

Julietta chuckled. "You're funny." She went to her room and checked her face in the mirror, ran a comb through her hair, and put on lip gloss. She grabbed her purse and her camera.

"Oh, good." Sofia pointed at the camera. "You definitely want to take pictures. Don't you have a camera on your smartphone though?"

"Yeah, I do. But the lens on the camera is better." She walked toward the door with Sofia following her.

"Have a great time," Sofia said and waved at Adam.

Adam and Julietta drove through the mountains to Highway One, then turned south and stopped at Harmony, the tiny village with a population of about eighteen people as it said on the town sign. As Julietta had read somewhere, the town of Harmony had once been a dairy settlement, established in the late nineteenth century by Swiss dairy farmers. In modern times, it had developed into an artist community. There were a few galleries and gift stores as well as a glassblowing workshop, a wedding chapel, and an old post office that was no longer in service.

Julietta took pictures and bought a T-shirt, wanting to support this unique place. Adam picked out a beautiful handmade ceramic bowl and gave it to Julietta as a present.

They drove north, stopped in Cambria to take a quick stroll through the quaint town, then continued toward Piedras Blancas, the elephant seal rookery near San Simeon.

Julietta was fascinated with these huge animals. As one of the guides explained to the tourists, July was the time when the young and adult males were shedding their fur and growing a new one, a process called "molting."

"And, being males, they of course have to yell at each other and fight over the ladies." Adam laughed, as they strolled along the bluff.

"Just like the human males," Julietta joked.

"Now, wait a minute," Adam protested, then shrugged. "I guess you have a point there." He began punching his chest and howled.

"Stop it." Julietta slapped his arm. Some people were staring at them.

"I'm sorry. I know. You can't take me anywhere."

They walked along a trail above the beach, admiring the huge animals and their occasional wrestling.

After taking pictures, they continued their drive north. Adam suggested they find out if the road to Big Sur was open, although he doubted it. As expected, the curvy mountain road was closed. They were able to drive just past Ragged Point, then had to turn back.

At Ragged Point they stopped. "It's not as dramatic as Big Sur, but it's pretty impressive, too," Adam said.

They walked along the path past the lodge and the gardens full of pink, purple, and blue flowers next to the stones and rocks in different shades of gray and black. Down at the bluff, they admired the stunning view of the Pacific. Julietta inhaled sharply as they stepped close to the abyss where the cliff dropped into the sea. "This is breathtaking, so beautiful," she whispered as they stood quietly, admiring the deep-blue water and the mountains to the north.

Adam smiled at her enthusiasm. "As beautiful as the Mediterranean?"

"Different," she said. "At least when compared to the sea close to Vignaverde. But there are places along the

Mediterranean that are similar. High cliffs, deep drops, and gorgeous beaches. But this is special. It's mysterious." She pointed to a few shreds of mist that rose from the sea.

"You know what I like most about this?" Adam said.

"What?" Julietta asked.

"We're here together," he said quietly. Julietta was struck by the intensity of his clear blue eyes. A patch of sunlight moved across his face and made them sparkle. He put his arms around her and brought his face closer to hers. Hesitating a brief moment, he kissed her gently, first on the cheek, then as she didn't pull back, he kissed her on the mouth.

Julietta closed her eyes and gave in to the warmth and the rush of energy through her body. She lost herself in the kiss that became more and more passionate, only to be interrupted by the sound of a twig or branch snapping and voices from other tourists approaching. They let go of each other, then walked, holding hands, toward the gardens in front of the motel.

Still overwhelmed by the sudden change in their relationship—they weren't simply friends anymore—Julietta asked herself what it all meant. She was in love, no doubt, with an American, just like her mother had been with her father. Would she and Adam end up in the same situation, struggling with a long-distance relationship? What if it didn't work out? Perhaps they'd have children and then what? She knew what it felt like being a child and only seeing her father once a year.

Julietta took a deep breath. She didn't want to think about the consequences right then. She wanted to enjoy the feeling of being in love and being loved. She loved Adam for his gentleness and his sense of humor.

"Let's sit down for a while," he said, interrupting her train of thought. He motioned in the direction of a wooden bench on the lawn.

He kissed her again. "You know, I've been in love with you for a while but never dared to make a move." He gently caressed a strand of Julietta's hair. "I guess I was worried what would happen if you left again for Italy. You know, after school."

Julietta nodded and squeezed his hand. "I was thinking the same thing. But perhaps we'll find a way if it works out between us. I mean perhaps I could stay here."

"Yes, or I could come to Italy with you."

"Have you ever been there? Or elsewhere in Europe?"

"Once with my parents. That was about five years ago. My father had some business dealings in Italy and he invited Mom and me to accompany him. We mainly saw the famous places such as Rome, Venice, Florence and a few more. I loved it. I even took Italian in school."

"Really? You never speak Italian with me." Julietta smiled at him.

"Oh, I'm too embarrassed. But you're right I need to practice again. We could take a trip there together, perhaps after graduating. I'd love to see Vignaverde and your vineyards there."

"Sounds perfect," Julietta said.

Chapter 10

"You're what?" Matthew glared at Marcia, his former girlfriend.

"I'm pregnant," she said. "And it could be yours."

Matthew felt the blood leave his face. "How is that possible? We always used protection." Matthew tried to steady his palpitating heart.

"Remember, once the condom broke?"

"Come on. One time and you even said it wasn't dangerous."

Marcia put one hand on her hip and ran the fingers of the other one through her short blond hair. "Well, I guess I was wrong."

"How would you even know it's mine? You had other boyfriends at the time. That's one of the reasons we broke up."

"Yes, but at that very time, you were the only one."

Thoughts were racing through Matthew's mind. *How could this be. This can't be.* "We need to do a paternity test. I want proof."

"That's all you're concerned about? You're such a cold bastard." She glared at him with her ice-blue eyes.

"I'm certainly not going to accept responsibility for a baby that isn't mine. Call me cold. I don't care. If it *is* mine, I'll take full responsibility. Whatever that means ... oh, God!"

"It'll be okay." Marcia came closer and put her arm on his. He pulled back.

Matthew had planned to do some shopping, but then he'd run into Marcia. After the devastating news, he'd lost interest and went home and straight to his computer. Still shaking inwardly, he began to search the Internet for paternity tests. He browsed a slew of them until one caught his attention. It was a prenatal test requiring a simple blood sample from the mother and, he assumed, from the potential father. The good thing was that it could be done as early as ten weeks into the pregnancy and it wasn't intrusive for the woman. It was ninety-nine percent accurate and, most importantly, you didn't have to wait until the baby was born.

As much as Matthew was afraid of the results, he wanted to know as soon as possible. He didn't want this hanging over his head. He picked up the phone and dialed Marcia's number. She didn't answer, instead the call went to voicemail, and he debated if he should leave a message. He didn't want anybody else to hear about their troubles, and he didn't know if Marcia lived alone. So he left a general message. "Marcia, the thing we talked about earlier today. I have a suggestion. Please call me." He left his number, then hung up.

He stepped to the window, gazing at the fading light of the evening sky and thought back to the two-year long relationship with Marcia. At first, he had been passionately in love with her. She was a vivacious and beautiful young woman. Sex had been fantastic, but after a while he noticed that she didn't take the relationship as seriously as he did. She had told him in the beginning of their dating that she didn't want to settle down with one man yet. He had been okay with it at first, but as time went on, he wanted them to be exclusive. She agreed, but when he caught her kissing another man, he knew they weren't on the same page with regard to their relationship. He got tired of what he felt was her "hot-and-cold syndrome," so he finally broke it off.

He should have done it sooner. Now, they were stuck in a mess. What could he do? If the baby was his, he'd have to pay. *God, I should've waited to buy the new car. But how was I supposed to know this could happen?*

After saving for several years, he had bought his dream car, a Porsche convertible. It was a secondhand car, but in good condition. What had made it easier for him to shell out the large sum of money was the fact that the car would increase in value over the years. But now, his savings were depleted, and he needed to build them up again. He might have to sell the car. He certainly didn't want his child to grow up poor. *My child? What am I thinking? How did it come to this?*

Matthew stepped outside. The sun had slipped down behind the horizon. It was still hot, but a light breeze stirred the small thick leaves on the live oak next to the house, which made a crackling sound as they rubbed against each other. A night bird was singing a sad tune. Matthew took a deep breath, trying to calm his nerves, but not even the peaceful environment was able to soothe his troubled heart.

A door opened at his parents' house next to his. He saw the silhouette of someone standing on the patio, then heard a cough. It was his father. Matthew stepped back into the shadow of the overhanging roof of his home. He didn't want to talk to anyone right then, least of all to his father.

On top of feeling like a failure at his job, he now felt like the biggest idiot. Getting a girl pregnant with all the birth control methods available, who had heard of such a thing? And it had to happen to him. Just another reason for his father to doubt him and his abilities.

Matthew massaged his throbbing forehead. "Calm down," he murmured. After all, it wasn't certain yet that he was the father. It didn't make sense. Would Marcia consider an abortion? He doubted it; she came from a good Catholic family. If it was true, if it was in fact his child, he would just have to deal with it, one way or another. Tears flooded his eyes.

"Please, God, help," he whispered. "What am I going to do?"

Chapter 11

"Matt, my office, please." Robert hollered across the hallway.

"What now?" he heard Matthew grumble. His son had been in a bad mood all day, blowing up at one of the workers, which was unusual. If Matt did blow up occasionally, it was at him, but he'd always treated members of the staff kindly.

"What's bugging you?" Robert asked as Matthew approached him with a gloomy face.

Matthew waved his hand dismissively. "Nothing. Just tired. Didn't sleep well last night."

"It's not going to take long," Robert said. "Where is Romero? Oh, here he is. Come on in."

Romero stepped into the office and gave Robert and Matthew a friendly smile.

"Why don't you guys sit down?" Robert motioned at the chairs. "I know it's late, but this is kind of important."

"What's the matter?" Matthew asked. He rubbed his eyes and suppressed a yawn.

"One of the workers alerted me to the fact that bottles of the Cabernet seem to be missing. Do you guys know anything about it?"

Romero and Matthew looked at each other.

"No," Matthew said.

Romero's facial expression darkened. He shook his head.

Robert glanced at a piece of paper on his desk. "He pulled some of the bottles and noticed that there seemed to be fewer boxes. He alerted Ken. Ken checked the paperwork and the inventory, and it looks like sixty bottles are missing."

"Gee, that's … odd." Matthew scratched his dark curly hair. "Could it be that they were misplaced? Remember we recently moved bottles to the new storage facility?"

Robert shrugged. "It's possible. I'm not alarmed yet. Anyway, what I would like you to do is search the property while I'm gone, and also double-check if any of the other varietals are missing."

"Where are you going again?" Matthew snapped.

Robert glared at him. He was getting tired of his son's moods. "What the fuck is wrong with you? I'm going to Chicago to visit some of our best clients. It's called customer support, in case you forgot. It's something you need to learn, too, if you want to go on selling wine. Next time, you come along."

Matthew's face turned dark red. "I apologize. Don't mind me. I got up on the wrong side of bed this morning."

"All right. Apology accepted. So, you guys are clear about what to do?"

"Yes," Romero said. "I'll go and check again. The bottles must be somewhere. I know I checked the inventory of the Cabs before I went on vacation, because I took care of the five hundred for the Marriott Hotel. At that time, all the bottles were there."

"Then they must have been moved or misplaced while you were away," Robert said to Romero. He knew that the manager had taken time off to take his sick daughter to a new clinic.

Romero nodded.

"How is Nora?" Robert asked.

Romero shrugged. "Not bad. The new treatment seems to help."

"Good," Robert said. "Keep me up to date and let me know if you need help."

"Thanks," Romero said in a low voice.

"What if we don't find the bottles?" Matthew asked.

"Well, there are several possibilities," Robert said. "Maybe there is some mistake in the paperwork, although I doubt it. Ken is a very meticulous accountant." He paused. "Or—and I don't want to believe this—somebody stole the wine."

"Jesus, you don't think …?" Matthew stared at him. "One of the employees?"

"I don't want to believe anything right now. Too early. Keep it quiet for the time being. I don't want to alert anyone. But do sporadic checks from now on. Write down anything unusual? Okay?"

Romero cleared his throat. "I'll definitely keep an eye open."

"Me, too, of course," Matthew said.

"Okay, that's it for the time being," Robert said. "Don't worry. I still think the wine has been misplaced."

Romero and Matthew stood up and walked toward the door. Robert thought about having a talk with Matthew, but his son was gone too fast. Instead, he turned to his manager.

"Romero?" Romero turned around and Robert motioned him to close the door and sit down again. Robert faced his friend and long-time employee. "As I said, I still hope the bottles will be found. But if not … and I hate to think about them being stolen, but you never know." He hesitated. "Just between you and me, can you think of anybody … you've known most of the people here for a long time, my family and the long-time employees. Can you think of anybody who'd steal wine?"

"Your family? You couldn't possibly think they would steal wine?"

"No, probably not." Robert sighed. "You know what's wrong with Matt? Why is he in such a crappy mood?"

"I'm sorry. I don't know." Romero looked at him puzzled. *Why am I asking my manager what's wrong with my son?* "Never mind. What about the employees? Do you think any of them would be capable of stealing wine?"

"None of the old-timers. The newer ones ... I don't know them well enough."

"What about Adam? You know, the kid who works here for the summer?"

"He seems like a nice person. I wouldn't think... Look, I really don't know."

Robert sensed he was making his manager very uncomfortable. Romero wouldn't want to accuse anybody without just cause. "I'm sorry," Robert said. "I shouldn't even ask you this. Let's forget it. Just keep your eyes open."

"Certainly," Romero said quietly and glanced at his watch.

"Sorry to keep you. It's much too late. Juanita is going to wonder what happened to you."

Romero gave a quick smile. "She isn't home. She and Nora went to visit her family."

"Oh, I see. Right. Well, Janice is out as well. So what are you doing for dinner? Wanna go and grab a bite?"

"Sorry, I can't tonight. Some other time perhaps?"

Robert nodded. "Okay. Good. See you after I get back from Chicago."

He didn't let on that he was disappointed. Romero and he had been friends for many years and had quite often gone out for dinner or drinks after work. This year, however, Romero had turned down almost every suggestion they do something together as friends, saying that he had other plans or was busy at home. Robert wondered if he had said or done anything to offend Romero, which would explain the increasing distance. He couldn't think of anything and their working relationship had always been cordial and didn't seem to have changed. Perhaps he read too much into Romero's behavior toward him. He knew that Romero was worried about his family and his daughter. He seemed to have aged and didn't look good. Robert decided to have a talk with him once he returned. There must be something Robert could do to help them.

He got up and stood next to the window, gazing at the large stretches of vineyards along the hills below the house. As peaceful and calm as the scenery looked, Robert couldn't help but feel uneasy, as if something dark was hiding underneath the veneer of beauty.

He hated the nagging suspicion that what happened on the estate wasn't simply a misplacement, that the wine bottles were stolen. But what was the purpose? Drinking the wine? More likely, selling it. The sale of stolen wine was a crime, plain and simple.

And there was the problem with Matthew. Their relationship seemed to be deteriorating. Matt and he had occasionally butted heads before. They were too similar, both strong-willed. A strong will wasn't a bad character trait in the business. His son, however, was resisting him all the time. After all, Robert was the one with the experience. Matt was a newbie. He was supposed to learn from his father rather than work against him. Had it been a mistake to take him into the business?

Robert shook his head, grabbed some papers he wanted to take with him and shoved them into his briefcase. *Time to go home and pack."*

Chapter 12

"I'll get it," Julietta called when she heard a knock on the door. Sofia was in the nursery getting little Henry up after his afternoon nap. Julietta was surprised to see Robert standing outside. She invited him in, and he followed her into the living room.

"Would you like something to drink?" she asked him. "Coffee? We also have some homemade lemonade."

"No, thank you. I just wanted to ask you a few questions." He sounded serious, even worried.

"Okay. Go ahead," Julietta sat on the couch and pointed at an easy chair.

Robert, however, remained standing. He shoved his hands into the front pockets of his jeans and glanced around the living room, then cleared his throat. "How well do you know Adam Winter? Are you two dating?"

Julietta was puzzled, not so much by Robert's question but by the curt, almost hostile tone. "Yes, we go out together. Why?"

"Well, I don't want to worry you. Adam looks like a nice person." Robert gave a quick smile and continued in a friendlier tone. "I'm just a little concerned because his uncle is a criminal. George Winter worked for the government and took bribes from vintners and winemakers in exchange for permits. A friend of mine and I found out about it and got him fired. As Adam told us, his uncle gave the family some wine from our estate. I cannot imagine him buying wine from us. We're not exactly friends. So if he didn't buy it, where did he get the wine? As you know bottles of Cabernet Sauvignon disappeared from our estate."

"I heard about the wine disappearing. But what do you mean, Uncle Robert?" Julietta asked. "You think Adam's uncle stole the wine?"

"Not he himself. I'm sure we'd have seen him, had he been on the estate. But perhaps someone he knew."

"You mean … Adam?" Julietta was stunned. "There is no way … I don't think he even knows where the wine is stored."

"Didn't you show him the storage facility when you gave him the tour initially?" Robert asked.

Julietta hesitated. "Yes, I did show him the building, but we didn't go inside … wait, that's not true. Ken went inside, checking something, so we took a peek. But Adam didn't give any indication he was investigating the wine or anything like that." Julietta's heart beat faster. She felt she was betraying Adam, although she was just being honest.

"Still, he knows where the wine is kept," Robert said. "The keys to the storage facility are on a hook in Ken's office where Adam works. He could easily take the keys and wait until after work or go there at night and remove a few bottles of wine at a time."

"Wouldn't somebody notice that the keys are missing?" Julietta asked.

"Not necessarily. Employees take them all the time when they need to fill an order," Robert said.

"That means anybody else could've taken the keys," Julietta said. "Not just Adam."

"True, and I'm not accusing him. I'm just concerned because of his background and connection to his uncle. It's just a strange coincidence that Adam asked you for a job at the winery when he realized you were related to me." He held up his hands, when Julietta began to protest.

"Look, I'm not saying Adam did anything wrong. I'm just a little uneasy, that's all. And I don't want you to get hurt," Robert added.

"Adam doesn't even like his uncle," Julietta said.

Robert nodded. "Yes, maybe I'm just being paranoid with all the stuff that's been going on lately, the misplaced or, possibly, stolen wine. Just be vigilant. I still hope we'll find the wine eventually." He smiled and turned toward Sofia, who had stepped into the living room, carrying little Henry.

"Hey, little man," Robert greeted Henry. He took him into his arms and tickled his chin. The baby, all excited, kicked with his short legs and gave a little shriek.

"I heard what you said about Adam," Sofia told Robert. "Do you really think he has something to do with the disappearing wine?"

Robert bounced Henry gently on his hip. "As I said, I don't know. I just wanted to let Julietta know about George Winter." He turned to Julietta. "Has Adam ever talked about his uncle?"

Julietta shook her head. "He just told me that his uncle gave them a bottle of wine as a present for his father's birthday, you know the same thing he told you in the tasting room. Since then we haven't talked about him. I don't think the two families, I mean his uncle and Adam's family, are close at all."

Robert nodded. "Just be careful. If you notice anything suspicious, I hope you'll let me know."

"Of course, why would I hide it from you?" Julietta was getting upset that Robert might think she would keep something important from him.

In the meantime, little Henry wanted attention. He wiggled in Robert's arms, rubbed his eyes, and started to cry.

"He's hungry. I'm going to feed him," Sofia said.

Robert handed her the baby and gently touched the little boy's cheek. Henry looked at him with big, tear-filled eyes, then gave a quick smile and started to cry again.

"See you later, Robert," Sofia said. She carried the child back to the nursery.

After Robert had left, Julietta went into the nursery and watched as Sofia fed the baby. Robert's suspicions saddened her. "I just don't believe Adam has anything to do with it. Robert is wrong. He makes me feel like he blames me for something."

"I don't think he blames you," Sofia said. "I think he's worried. And he can be abrupt sometimes."

Julietta nodded. "It just makes me feel unhappy. I really like Adam. I can't imagine him having an ulterior motive when he asked me for a job at the estate. He seems so open and honest."

"But you haven't known him that long yet."

"No, but don't you think I'd notice if he just pretended to like me?"

"I'm sure, you're right," Sofia said.

Julietta stared at her. "You don't think Robert is right ... or do you?"

"No ... I don't know Adam very well, but he seems like a nice man." Sofia touched Julietta's arm. "But I don't want you to get hurt either. Don't rush into a close relationship. Take it slow."

"You don't sound very encouraging," Julietta said sadly. "Well, classes are going to start soon again. We'll both be busy next quarter, and Adam is going to do an internship out of town. So we probably won't see that much of each other next term."

"Well, I really hope things work out with Adam and you. I like him."

"Yeah, I do, too. But all this talk about the stolen or misplaced wine and his criminal uncle is not very encouraging. I hope they'll find the wine or who took it fast."

"I hope so, too," Sofia said. "I hate when something like this happens. It makes everybody suspicious and really pollutes the atmosphere."

Chapter 13

"Coming, coming, little troublemaker." Nicholas groaned, as he got up. Two-month old Henry had started to cry at the crack of dawn, demanding breakfast.

Sofia rolled over and yawned, then sat up in bed and glanced out the window. The early daylight covered the landscape with a purplish hue. A slight morning breeze shook the top of the wisteria vine in front of the house. She pulled off her T-shirt and got ready to breastfeed their baby. For the past couple of weeks, Henry had slept through the night occasionally, which gave the parents a short time of peace. He was, however, up early in the mornings.

"Our own human alarm clock," Nicholas called him. He went to pick up the little boy and put him on the bed next to Sofia, who proceeded to feed him. Yawning loudly, Nicholas went to shower and dress.

Sofia enjoyed this first relaxing feeding time. She kissed Henry, who sucked and grunted. The scent of freshly brewed coffee mingling with the sweet baby smell brought a smile to Sofia's face.

A while later, Nicholas opened the door and brought in a cup, putting it on the nightstand next to Sofia. He picked up Henry who had almost fallen asleep and carried him around to burp him. After changing his diaper, he brought him back and put him next to Sofia again. He kissed them both.

"Thanks, honey, you're such a great daddy." Sofia took a sip of coffee, enjoying the invigorating, slightly bitter taste.

Nicholas grinned. "Okay, you two lazy bums, Daddy is off to work."

"I'll join you later," Sofia called after him. Nicholas left for his early morning walk through the vineyards.

With Henry sleeping again, Sofia allowed herself to doze for ten more minutes. Then she got up, put the little boy back into his crib, and went to take a shower. She wanted to join Nicholas and Martin in the vineyards. As much as she enjoyed her new role of mother, she didn't want to give up her work at the winery. Besides, they needed the money, having made a somewhat rash decision to buy a new house. The mortgage turned out to be more of a burden than they had anticipated. Fortunately, Sofia still had her freelance writing job for a culinary magazine that brought in some extra cash.

Nicholas had initially suggested they hire a nanny part-time, but the whole family had protested that it wasn't necessary, that enough people would help take care of little Henry, the newest member of the Segantino clan. Janice and Maria and even Matthew and Martin volunteered. During vacation and on weekends, Julietta helped out and so did Nadia, Nicholas and Matthew's younger sister, when she was home from UC Davis. Even her aunt, Emma, her father's sister who lived in Santa Monica, came up and spent a few days, spoiling her great-nephew.

Sofia, who had grown up in a very small family with only her father and her aunt enjoyed the extended family of the Segantinos. Even as a child she had always wanted a sibling. When she found out about Julietta, her father's other daughter in Italy he had kept hidden from her, it took some time for her to be able to forgive him for having withheld that family secret. Later, her sense of having been betrayed gave way to gratitude when she met her sister.

Sofia hummed as she combed her blond-highlighted, light-brown hair. She had cut her long hair during the pregnancy and now wore it in a modern bob. She applied a light eye shadow that accentuated her purple-blue eyes and added some lip gloss. Still trying to shed some extra weight from her pregnancy, she decided to walk to her in-laws' home. She was tall and had been very slim, but now her hips and her belly still carried those pesky pounds.

The rather steep path up the hill to Robert and Janice's property was perfect for exercise and getting her heart pumping. She put little Henry in his front carrier, strapped him to her body, and grabbed the bag with extra diapers, a few prepared bottles of milk, and toys.

On top of the hill, Sofia stopped, catching her breath. She looked around, enjoying the view of the valley. The fields of yellow sun-dried grasses and dark green live oaks stretched to the horizon. Sofia scrunched her eyes as she watched a black bird—a raven perhaps—soaring above the trees.

She caught a glimpse of Robert through the window of his office on the first floor of his home. The door to the house was ajar and she heard some agitated voices. "Uncle Matthew is here, too," she told her son.

"And you didn't think it necessary to let me, to let us know?" Matthew's voice sounded irritated.

"Matt, calm down, it's just a stupid anonymous scribble. Who knows it may be the Water Queen. You know she's nuts. Whoever it is, I'm not going to give them the satisfaction of reacting to it."

Sofia had heard of the woman activist who had protested in front of wineries with a few of her friends, denouncing the vintners' "raping of the land and wasting water." She was considered a little unbalanced.

"Dad, you don't know. It may be serious. Don't you think someone is out to harm you?"

"Stop blowing it out of proportion. This belongs in the trashcan."

Sofia knocked on the half-open door and pushed it open all the way. As she stepped inside, Robert tossed a piece of paper into the wastepaper basket. Robert got up, and Matthew turned around, and their tense facial expressions gave way to smiles.

"Hey, my favorite nephew," Matthew said and tickled Henry's chin. Henry gurgled and waved his arms.

Sofia lifted Henry out of his cloth seat and handed Robert the baby. "Coming to see your Grandpa, huh?" Robert held and kissed the little boy.

"What were you two guys arguing about? I couldn't help overhearing something about an anonymous letter," Sofia asked.

Robert sat down and bounced little Henry on his knee. He waved his hand in a dismissive gesture. "Nothing to worry about."

"Well, here it is. What do you think?" Matthew fished the piece of paper out of the wastepaper basket and handed it to Sofia.

It was a typed letter. Sofia scrunched her forehead as she read it.

I warned you before. This is my last warning. Stop wasting water. Stop poisoning people with alcohol or you and your family will regret it!

"Gee, that sounds nasty. What does this mean?" Sofia asked.

Matthew glared at his father. "Is this the first one you received? It says here 'my last warning,' so there were others?"

Robert shrugged. "I got a couple of them before."

"F—" Matthew caught himself and glanced at Henry. "I don't understand how you can ignore this." He ran his fingers through his hair. His already sun-tanned face had darkened. "Well, anyway, I have to get back to work." He walked toward the door. "See you later," he said to Sofia, then left.

Robert gave a weak smile. "He takes things too seriously."

"Well, we're off, too," Sofia said. "Janice is waiting."

Robert kissed Henry, then handed him to Sofia. He picked up her bag for her. "I'll see you guys in a while."

Sofia hesitated. She knew that Robert could be stubborn, and she didn't want to anger him. She took a deep breath. "Perhaps you should do something about the letter, just to be on the safe side."

Robert nodded. "I'll show it to Walt Smith," he said, referring to the sheriff who was a friend of Robert's.

"Does Janice know?" Sofia asked.

"No, I don't want to worry her. I'd appreciate it if you didn't say anything."

Sofia nodded. "Okay, I won't tell her." She felt Robert was avoiding a serious issue.

Chapter 14

It was another busy day at the estate. Sofia walked into the living room of her home in shorts and a T-shirt. She was getting ready to go to the winery. "You're sure, it's not too much trouble, watching him?" she asked her sister.

"Of course, not." Julietta said. "I love babysitting him. Besides, he's asleep most of the time. Don't worry."

"I just don't want to overburden you. Don't you have studying to do?" Sofia grabbed her sun hat and a bottle of water.

"Hey, it's vacation time. Besides, I finished whatever studying I had to do."

"Okay, I'm really grateful," Sofia said and opened the door. "Oh, look who's here." Curious, Julietta joined her.

Adam, walking up to the house, waved at them and Julietta felt her face stretch into a smile.

"Hello, ladies," he greeted them. "You look beautiful today … well, of course, any day."

Sofia laughed. "I'm sure you came for Julietta. I'm off to work." She winked at Julietta and left.

"Come inside." Julietta put a finger on her lips. "Shhh. The baby is still asleep."

Adam tiptoed into the living room.

Julietta grinned. "You can walk normally. He doesn't wake up easily. Just don't scream or something."

"Scream? Why would I scream? Now, listen, what are you planning to do to me that would make me scream?" He wiggled his eyebrows.

She playfully hit his arm, then led him into the nursery where little Henry was asleep, his arms stretched over his head, his pudgy cheeks slightly flushed.

"Cute little guy," Adam whispered.

"He is, isn't he?" Julietta said. "Want some coffee?"

They went into the living room and Julietta got them two cups of espresso from the kitchen and a plate of cookies. "Are you done with work for the day?"

"Yes. Ken had to leave early, and we're pretty much caught up with the daily data entry and the filing, so he gave me the time off. I think the poor guy is having relationship or family problems. I heard him arguing on the phone, maybe with his wife. It sounded pretty ugly."

"Oh? What were they arguing about?" Julietta asked.

"Not sure," Adam said. "I didn't hear the whole thing. I was in the filing room, just heard a few sentences, but I think it was about money."

"Too bad," Julietta said. "Ken seems like such a nice man."

"Yeah, he's really nice. Perhaps a little too nice, you know, the kind of guy that lets himself be pushed around. Just got that feeling." Adam shrugged. "But anyway. Are you babysitting tonight?"

"No, just for a couple of hours this afternoon. Why?"

"Have you ever been to one of those free concerts in the downtown park?" Adam asked.

"Yes, once with my sister and brother-in-law. It was fun."

"Would you be interested in going tonight? That friend of mine I mentioned before, the one who plays saxophone in a jazz band, is on tonight. They're really good. They even played at the Hearst Castle a few times."

"Whoa. Sounds interesting. I love jazz."

"Good." Adam's face lit up. "As you know, it's very casual. Perhaps we could have a bite to eat afterward?"

"Yes, why not?"

"Good, I'll pick you up at five o'clock, if that's all right." Adam touched her arm.

"Wonderful." Julietta's heartbeat picked up speed. At that moment, they were interrupted by the sound of crying.

"Oh, oh. Someone is calling for you. Another young man. Almost makes me jealous," Adam joked.

Julietta laughed. She went to pick up the little boy and brought him into the living room. He had stopped crying and Adam gently touched his cheek. "My competition. But I can't blame you. He's so cute."

"You're silly." Julietta smiled.

"I know. Anyway, I'll pick you up later. Okay?"

"Yes, thanks Adam. Looking forward to it." Julietta watched him leave.

He sure was a charmer. Julietta was happy to have something to look forward to. She had talked to her mother on the phone that morning. Afterward, she had felt a little homesick. Although she loved living in California, it was the first time she had been away from home so long.

At five o'clock, Adam drove them to downtown Paso Robles. They parked on one of the side streets near the park.

"I'm still surprised how easy it is to find a parking spot here. It's a real challenge in San Luis Obispo," Adam said.

"That's one of the advantages of a small town," Julietta said. "It does get more crowded though during the wine festival."

Grabbing two lawn chairs and their water bottles, they made their way into the park. It was fairly crowded already but they found a place not too far from the gazebo, where the band would be playing.

"Care for something to drink?" Adam asked.

Julietta nodded. Adam walked across the lawn toward the stand with the beverages. Julietta looked around. She didn't see anybody she knew. She was sitting back comfortably, waiting for Adam, when she felt someone watching her. A heavyset man, standing a few feet away, was staring at her. He was holding what looked like a bottle of beer. His face was shadowed by the brim of his baseball cap, but Julietta could tell he was observing her.

"Here you are." Adam gave her a glass of lemonade and sat down on the lawn chair. "It's pretty crowded at the beverage stand. I guess that's good for business."

"Thanks," Julietta said and took a sip of her lemonade. She glanced in the direction of the man she'd seen before, but he seemed to have disappeared. Perhaps, she had been wrong. He may have been looking at someone else.

After a while, the band went on stage and Adam pointed out his friend Jonathan, a skinny, young man with a blond ponytail and a saxophone.

The band played for half an hour, then took a short break. Julietta admitted they were very good. During the break, Adam and Julietta walked toward the stage. Jonathan waved and came down to greet Adam, who introduced Julietta. They walked over to the beverage stand and got another glass of lemonade each. After talking for a while, Jonathan headed toward the stage and Adam and Julietta went back to their seats.

"Well, well," a dark voice said behind them as they sat down. "It's my nephew with a beautiful girl he never told me about."

Julietta turned around and looked into the face of the man she had seen staring at her before.

"Uncle George, what are you doing here?" Adam said.

"Same as you, enjoying the music." The man stepped closer and Julietta smelled the booze on his breath. "Aren't you going to introduce me to the pretty lady?"

"Oh, sorry, this is Julietta. Julietta, this is my uncle George."

Julietta didn't let on that she was bewildered. Here was the man Robert had warned her about, the one he had caused to lose his job because of some illegal activities while he was working for the county government. She had taken an immediate dislike to him, even before Adam introduced him. His lascivious glances, as if he wanted to undress her, and the smell of alcohol on his breath made her feel sick. Adam, however, didn't seem to feel uncomfortable around him.

"Julietta is the sister of Sofia Segantino, one of the owners of the estate. Remember you brought us some wine from them once?" Adam explained. "I'm working at the estate during the summer."

A rush of emotions flashed over the man's face, anger perhaps or confusion, it was difficult to make out. It lasted only a second and then he smiled again, but the smile seemed fake. "Oh, yes," he said. "Pretty decent wine." He pushed his cap back. "So, how do you like the work there?" he asked Adam, looking at him quizzically, then back at Julietta.

"It's great," Adam said. He put his hand on Julietta's shoulder.

"Good, good to hear," George said in a low voice. "Well, I got to go. I'm meeting a friend." He slapped Adam on the back. "Good to see you. Say hello to the family." He turned to Julietta. "Very nice meeting you." He put his finger to his cap in a salute, then turned around and left.

Julietta heaved a sigh of relief. The man had given her the creeps. Adam watched his uncle walk across the lawn. He chortled. "Some character."

It didn't sound as if he disliked him. He seemed rather amused by his uncle. "Well, now you've met the black sheep of our family." He chortled.

"He is a little strange," Julietta said, careful not to offend Adam.

"That he is," Adam agreed. "He isn't a bad guy, just a troublemaker. Unfortunately, one of his problems is alcohol. I think he was pretty loaded already." He pointed to the stage. "Anyway, enough about Uncle George. Here's the band again."

After the concert, they went to a restaurant that served tapas and other kinds of Spanish food. They sat outside on the patio, enjoying the warm evening, talking about the concert. In spite of the pleasant and relaxing atmosphere, Julietta kept thinking back to the surprise meeting with Adam's uncle. She thought of Robert's misgivings and his veiled suspicions that Adam might have an ulterior and perhaps damaging motive for working at the Segantino estate. Robert hadn't given her any details, so she didn't know what the background of his animosity toward George Winter was, except that Robert had been instrumental in the latter losing his job.

She wondered if she should ask Adam what he knew about his uncle. But she didn't want to spoil the pleasant and relaxing atmosphere and the deepening relationship between them, a relationship she welcomed but feared as well. Feared, not just because of the suspicions Robert had of him but because of other uncertainties. If they became a couple, where would they live in the future? Here or in Italy? She thought of her mother and her father, the constant separations, the pain of having to always say good-bye to her father, his sudden, unexpected death. It was something she and Adam had briefly talked about but neither one of them knew the answer.

What would happen if she stayed here? She liked living with Sofia and Nicholas, and she loved her little nephew. But at the same time, she would miss her mother, her Italian family, and her friends at home.

Why was she even worrying about something so uncertain? What was the English saying about that? *Counting your chickens before they hatch?*

She sensed Adam's eyes on her and looked at him.

"You're deep in thought," he said.

Julietta smiled and shook her head. "Just enjoying the evening."

Chapter 15

Nicholas slowly made his way between the rows of vines. It was dawn, the perfect time to get some work done before the heat set in. His grandfather used to do it every day, rain or shine, but now, the seventy-six-year-old man skipped a day once in a while, nursing an occasional bout of arthritis. But most of the time, he would be there, hiking on the soft sandy soil between the rows of vines. It was more difficult to walk on sand than on grass, but long before the drought became an urgent problem, Martin Segantino had decided to conserve water. Grass needed to be watered more often than the vines, so it didn't make sense to plant it between the rows and waste water that way.

Nicholas loved these early morning walks together with his grandfather. It gave them time to talk about family, work, the community. Often, they would walk in silence and to Nicholas it felt like a meditation. At the same time, it was an important part of the work. They checked the vines to make sure no pests or disease were present. Fortunately, the climate in the Paso Robles area was too dry for the kind of infestation that threatened the vines in more humid areas of the country.

Today, however, Nicholas was alone. His grandparents were away for a few days, visiting friends. Halfway through the vineyards, he took a break, drank a few sips of water from the bottle he carried with him, and watched the sun rise above the horizon and color the fields golden. He inhaled the scent of sage. The early morning breeze rustled the dry grass next to the vineyard. Two crows sitting on the fence cawed.

Every so often, small animals, rabbits and squirrels, scampered by him. Feeling someone watching him, he turned around and was faced with a coyote, staring at him. They observed each other for a moment, then the animal turned and slunk away through the tall yellow grass. Up in the sky, hawks drew circles, watching for prey.

About an hour later, Nicholas returned home. As he opened the door, the scent of freshly brewed coffee lured him into the kitchen. Sofia, holding a fussing Henry in her arms, was trying to crack open the eggs. Nicholas smiled, kissed her, and took the baby in his arms, cuddling him.

"Thanks, just in time," Sofia said. She poured two cups of coffee and proceeded to break open the eggs. Strips of bacon were sizzling in the frying pan. Nicholas kissed Sofia's neck, grabbed a cup and took a few sips, then put the cup down. He carried Henry around, who promptly fell asleep again. Nicholas gently put him back into the crib.

"What's the occasion for this rich breakfast?" Nicholas carried the plates with the eggs and bacon to the table.

"You need something solid in your stomach after getting up so early … and I'm sick and tired of my healthy cereal." Sofia gave him a warning look as if to say, "Don't you dare mention my wanting to lose weight."

Nicholas had no intention of saying anything of that sort. In fact, he liked the love handles Sofia had left over from her pregnancy. "Honey, thank you, this is a real treat for a hard-working peasant."

"Ha ha." Sofia grinned. "How are the vines doing?"

"Perfect," Nicholas, said. "The Sangiovese should be ready to harvest in a couple of weeks."

With breakfast over, Nicholas grabbed a handful of mail from the basket next to the front door. He separated the bills from the other mail and sat down at the table again. Staring at the pile of bills, he sighed, then got up, went into the kitchen and poured himself another cup of coffee. Sitting back down, he groaned.

"What's the matter?" Sofia asked. She was reclined on the sofa, breastfeeding Henry. Nicholas leaned back in his chair, then sat straight up again and motioned at the papers in front of him. "Bills, bills, bills. Perhaps we should've listened to Grandpa's warning before buying the house."

"Are we in trouble?" Sofia's voice shook a little.

"Not in deep trouble," Nicholas said. "It's just, we don't seem to get ahead. We had a great harvest two years ago. The one last year was fine, not great. I just wish we could've had a larger down payment. The mortgage is killing us."

Sofia got up, carrying Henry on her shoulder, trying to burp him. She came over to Nicholas and watched him sort through the bills. "Hmm. Perhaps I should accept more freelance work," she suggested.

"No, Sofia, you have enough to do with the baby and helping us at the winery. I think we'll be okay. Just have to tighten our belts for a while."

"That's okay," Sofia said. "Perhaps, we could refinance and borrow a larger down payment from the family. They'd help."

"No, I don't want to borrow money from the relatives. Id' feel embarrassed." Nicholas slapped one of the bills on the table. "I guess I'm too proud to admit having been a little reckless. You know Grandpa suggested we wait until we had more of a down payment. Of course, he was right. We were just too impatient."

"It's probably my fault," Sofia said. "I fell in love with the house, and if we hadn't taken it when it was available, someone else might have snatched it up."

Sofia let her eyes wander over the living room of their dream house with the hardwood floor, covered by a few colorful rugs, the large floor to ceiling windows and sliding glass doors, the breakfast nook in the corner next to the open kitchen with the island, the walls with their light wood paneling.

"It's not your fault. I loved the house as much as you did. Still do. We'll be okay." Nicholas got up and kissed Henry. "You love it, too, don't you," he cooed. "Having your own nursery and a nice large yard, once you're big enough to walk and enjoy it."

The baby made gurgling sounds and grabbed Nicholas's chin. "See, he agrees," he said.

"Time for his diaper change." Sofia kissed Nicholas. "Don't worry. It'll work out, you'll see." She got ready to carry Henry to the nursery.

"I know," Nicholas said. "Anyway, time for me to do some work and get my mind off finances." He picked up the bills and shoved them back into the box for the current mail. "See you later," he called. He opened the door and left.

While Nicholas was at the winery, Sofia took advantage of Henry's second nap of the morning, poured herself another cup of coffee, and stepped onto the patio. The sun had risen but it was still cool enough for a few moments to enjoy the outside. Sofia gazed at the fields around her, burnt by the hot summer. The air smelled of lavender from the shrub at the edge of the patio.

She took a deep breath and closed her eyes. A lot of work with the baby and the estate as well as short nights, interrupted by Henry's early wake-up calls, didn't leave much time to relax. Soon she would take the little boy to his great-grandma Maria and join Nicholas at the winery. There was an outright competition between the family members as to who got to babysit Henry. Sofia was grateful for the love and attention she received from her in-laws, her own family having dwindled to her aunt and her grandparents.

The jingle of her cell phone interrupted the quiet. It was her grandmother on her father's side in Vermont, checking in on her and her great-grand baby.

"What a coincidence," Sofia said. "I was just thinking of you." They talked for a while and Sofia promised to visit with Henry soon. They exchanged the latest news and her grandmother thanked her for the pictures Sofia and Nicholas had sent over the Internet. Both her paternal grandparents were too old to travel much anymore. But her grandmother loved social media and was on Facebook almost every day.

As appreciative as Sofia was for her in-laws, she sometimes regretted the fact that she couldn't share her little boy more with her own side of the family. She missed her father. He would have been such a wonderful grandfather to his little namesake. Fortunately, her father-in-law was a good grandpa to little Henry. It warmed her heart to see how the usually impatient and often curt Robert was loving and tender with his first grandchild.

Sofia didn't have many memories of her mother, a woman who had suffered from bipolar disorder and ended up killing herself with an overdose of drugs when Sofia was twelve years old. She had very few happy memories of her mother. It was really her aunt Emma who had raised her and had become her mother.

Her father had been not only her parent but also her best friend. When she found out that he had led a double life, had had a lover in Tuscany and fathered a daughter, she had been deeply disappointed by his lack of honesty. As upsetting and tumultuous that time had been, it had also enriched her life.

She now had a sister, something she had always wished for. And now Julietta was with her in California, which made Sofia very happy.

Chapter 16

Robert was going through some papers in his office when the phone rang. He picked it up and answered with his usual curt "Yep. What's the matter?"

"Excuse me? Is this the Segantino estate?" a male voice said.

Robert checked the display and noticed that it was an external call. "I'm sorry. I thought it was an internal call. Yes, this is the Segantino Winery. How can I help you?"

"Hi there. My name is Sam Heller from the Wine Boutique in Solvang. I had ordered some of your wine in the past from one of your agents. I wanted to place another order, but I can't get a hold of the man. I get a 'number not in service' message."

"Oh?" Robert said, baffled. "What was the name of the agent? We don't really work with agents, at least not in the United States, just with restaurants or stores directly."

"Really? How odd. Well, the name was Santori, Fred, yes, Fred Santori. I had written it down."

Robert hesitated. "I don't know anybody by that name. But let me check with my manager. When did you say you ordered the wine?"

"About a month ago. Yeah, here it is, on July 5. It was a special deal, as he mentioned. I ordered several bottles of Cabernet. I liked the wine a lot and, as I said, I wanted to order more."

"Okay," Robert said. "I'm happy you liked it. Listen, let me call you back. I just want to double-check the order with my manager and accountant. Just make sure, we work with a Santori."

"Do you think there is something wrong with the order? It sounded like a legitimate sale. I'm usually careful about checking the source, but since this was a special deal, I just accepted."

"I don't blame you at all. I just want to make sure everything is okay. Give me your number and I'll call you right back. Oh, I have your number on my display." Robert repeated the phone number.

"Yes, that's fine," the man said.

"Great, Mr. Heller."

"Call me Sam."

"Okay, Sam, I'll be in touch." Robert disconnected. He stared at the wall for a while, trying to make sense of this odd phone call. Something very strange was going on, something very wrong, something that might explain the disappearing wine. Did someone sell stolen wine under his name and label?

He called Ken on the phone and asked him to come to his office, then stepped into the hallway and waved to Romero, who came walking toward him.

"Where's Matt?" he asked.

"I think he's in the cellar, fixing a leaking hose," the manager said.

"Why is *he* fixing the hose? Can't one of the workers do it?" Robert barked annoyed.

Romero shrugged, then hurried toward the door to the winery. "I'll get him."

A few minutes later, Romero came back with Matthew in tow.

"What are you doing, fixing a hose?" Robert asked, irritated. "I've told you before you don't have to do all the grunt work. There're enough workers who can take care of that."

Matthew glared at him. "Everybody was busy, so I did it myself. What's the big deal?"

Robert waved his hand dismissively. "Never mind. We've other things to talk about. He walked back into his office and motioned to the men to come in. "Close the door and sit down." He pointed at the chairs. "We got a new problem. A serious one."

"What's going on?" Matthew asked.

Three pairs of worried eyes looked at Robert. "I just got a troubling phone call." He told them about the wine merchant who had wanted to order more wine but couldn't find the so-called agent who had sold it to him in the first place.

"Have any of you heard of a man by the name of Fred Santori?"

The three men shook their heads and stared at him, puzzled. "We don't have any agents, do we? At least not for sales in the United States," Matthew said. "Only direct clients."

"That's right," Robert said. "But someone in this country must be posing as an agent of our estate and selling our wine illegally."

"Jesus," Ken said. "Is that where the disappearing wine bottles went?" He stared at Romero and Matthew.

"But then who is Fred ... what's his name? Santori?" Romero asked, his voice tense.

"I bet it's a fake name," Robert said. "Sam Heller, the wine merchant who just called me, said that the phone number he received and tried to call was either false or disconnected. Besides, as far as I know we never sold anything to Sam Heller at the Wine Boutique. Right, Ken?"

Ken scratched his forehead. "I don't think so. I'd have to double-check the records to see if he's in our wine club or if we ever sold him anything."

"Well, even if we did, we would have sold it to him directly," Matthew said. "And not through some unknown agent."

"As much as I hate to say it. It looks like someone is stealing bottles of our wine and selling them." Robert scratched his head.

The other three men exchanged stunned looks.

"Has anybody noticed anything unusual?" asked Robert. "Even if it sounds insignificant, it may lead to something."

More shaking heads and puzzled faces.

"Do you mean …?" Matthew swallowed hard. "Someone on the estate is doing this?"

Robert measured him thoughtfully. "What else could it be? Unless someone from outside can walk through the estate without raising suspicions." He glanced at Ken. "What do you think of Adam?"

Ken looked surprised. "How do you mean? He does a good job, is very helpful, seems like a nice guy. Why?"

"Just a thought." Robert didn't want to raise suspicions without having proof. "I'm afraid I'll have to get the authorities involved. It could even become a matter for the Bureau of Alcohol, Tobacco, Firearms, and Explosives. In the meantime, let's pay attention and be vigilant. If you hear or see anything, let me know."

"Yes, of course," Matthew said.

Robert stood. The other three men did the same and started toward the door. "Romero? One moment," Robert said.

Romero stopped at the door. After the other two had left, Robert walked up to him. "You seem very gloomy. Something wrong with Nora?"

Robert was shocked to see tears well up in Romero's eyes. "Yes. She had another attack last night." His voice broke.

"I'm so sorry. Listen, if there's anything I can do, let me know, please."

Romero nodded. "Yes, I know. We're grateful for your help, but all we can do right now is wait and see."

"Give my regards to Juanita and Nora," Robert said, putting a hand on Romero's shoulder.

Romero nodded, gave a weak smile, and left.

Robert sat down at his desk and stared into space. He was truly worried now. When they first noticed the missing bottles of Cabernet, he hoped they had been misplaced. Now, however, it was clear the wine was stolen.

But who? And when did it all start? He had been told about the missing bottles a month ago, but that's when one of the workers first discovered it. Sam Heller's order, however, went back to the fifth of July, so it could have started earlier in the year without anybody noticing. They only did a thorough inventory at the end of the year, and unless a large number of bottles went missing all at once, it could have stayed under the radar.

Robert pressed his fingers against his forehead and rubbed his temples. What bothered him more was the question of who? It must have been someone with access to the storage facility. During the day, quite a few people of his staff had access. At night and on weekends, the storage facility was locked. There was no sign of a break-in. After the regular working hours, some of the long-time employees and members of his family had keys.

What was worse was the fact that the wine was being sold. If someone had taken some wine for his or her own consumption, that would have been one thing. It would have been bad enough and certainly a theft. But that could have been dealt with internally. But wine being sold illegally was a crime. Robert hated to get the police involved, but he had no choice.

He picked up the phone and called Romero. "Make a list of all the people you know of who have access to the storage facility during the day and who have a key for it after work … including members of my family."

There was silence, then Romero. "Members of the family? You don't think …"

"No, probably not, but I want to cover all the bases. And, Romero, keep it quiet for right now."

"Certainly," Romero said. He sounded dejected.

No wonder. Whatever way they looked at it. The peace of the estate was shattered. Exhaling deeply, Robert called Walt Smith, the sheriff. He explained the situation. Walt told him he would contact the ATF and try to find someone who had experience with crimes involving wine.

The following morning, Robert found two lists with names on his desk, one of them with members of the daytime staff who had access to the storage room and the cellar. It included about twenty people. The second list contained the persons who had a key and access during non-working hours. It listed the longtime employees and all his family members. Romero's name was on top of the list.

Robert gave a quick chuckle, then added his own name on top of Romero's.

Chapter 17

Romero didn't really feel like meeting his friends for a guys' evening out, but he also felt too restless to stay home. He was upset about the upheaval caused by the wine theft and illegal sale. Guilt haunted him; this should've never happened under his watch. Exhaling deeply, he stared out the window at the fields of vines in front of his house. The ripe grapes, almost ready for the harvest that normally gladdened him, now made him feel miserable. Better go out after all, he thought. Otherwise, he'd be pacing the whole evening and wouldn't be able to settle down. At least he could have a few drinks. Of course, he wouldn't be able to forget the whole calamity, but the alcohol might numb the pain and guilt somewhat. Amazing, he thought, how fast an innocent pleasure could turn into an addiction. He felt his wife's eyes on him.

"I'm off," Romero said. "I may be late. Don't wait up for me." He picked up his wallet from the table.

"You look elegant." Juanita smiled at him and raised an eyebrow. Romero was dressed in slacks and a light-blue button-down shirt. "You sure you're getting together with a bunch of male friends and not some pretty women?"

"Silly goose," Romero said. "I'm not interested in pretty women. A beautiful Juanita is quite enough for me." He kissed her and forced a smile.

Juanita gently touched his arm. "I just hope they'll solve the puzzle soon, and you can relax again.

"It's my fault," he said. "I wish I could just make it go away. The whole thing is very upsetting."

"Does Robert blame you?"

"No, but that doesn't change the fact that I'm the manager and ultimately responsible. I should've been more careful."

"Romero, he's the owner. He should've paid attention, too."

"No, Juanita. He depends on me for running the estate."

"Perhaps he shouldn't be gone so much. It's unfair to have you run the whole estate with so little help."

"Matthew helps," Romero said. "And the rest of the staff. Look, whatever way you turn it, it's a real mess."

"I just hope it's not someone from the estate, doing all this."

Romero nodded. He looked at his watch. "I better go."

Juanita patted his shoulder. "Go and have a good time with your friends. And forget about the whole thing for a while. It will be resolved one way or the other, you'll see."

"One way or the other. Either way will be a disaster." His voice trembled. He gave a quick wave and left.

Juanita followed him to the door and watched as he walked to the car. He was hunched over, as if he carried the world on his back. Why did he take it so hard? He had been troubled for weeks, more than usual. She attributed it to his being worried about Nora. He shouldn't be worried about the estate that much. Yes, he was the manager, but he worked hard. Other people needed to help shoulder the burden. She liked Robert, he had been very generous with them, but she wasn't the only one who felt he should be more directly involved in the estate. She'd heard the same complaints from Matthew and even Janice.

As if her thoughts about the owner's wife had conjured her up, Janice turned the corner at the bottom of the driveway and was walking toward the house. Juanita waved at her.

She invited Janice inside and told her to sit down. "May I offer you something to drink?" Juanita asked. "We just opened a bottle of Sangiovese for dinner."

"Thank you. I won't say no," Janice said. "Where's Nora?"

"She is staying over at a friend's place for a few days."

"Ah, the one with the pool and the ponies?"

"Yes. She was really excited, and she gets to ride their ponies." Juanita smiled as she poured them each a glass of wine.

"That's such a great idea. That way, she can get around even though she isn't able to walk," Janice said.

"Exactly. And it's healthy for her. The whole family takes a bunch of trips, mainly to Lake Nacimiento. They ride their ponies and go swimming. Last year, though, the lake didn't have enough water. This year it's better."

"How wonderful. You know, we should get a pony for her to ride around here. We'd have enough room and there is an old shed, you know the one behind your home, we could turn into a stable." Janice sounded exited.

Juanita laughed. "Well, yes, that would be great. The problem is, someone would have to take care of the animal, and with everybody being so busy … I guess I could do it. We used to have a horse at my parents' house."

"See? I'll talk to Robert. I'm sure it would be possible."

"I don't know, Janice. With the troubles the estate seems to have right now, a pony might not be Mr. Segantino's primary goal."

"Just leave it up to me," Janice said with a smile, then became serious. "You're right though, we do have some issues with the stolen wine and the illegal sale."

Juanita sighed. "Romero takes it real hard. He feels it's his fault for not having noticed that something was wrong."

"Oh, come on, he shouldn't feel bad," Janice said. "None of the other staff and not even Robert noticed it. When they first realized bottles were missing, they thought that perhaps they were misplaced. It was only when one of the merchants called that Robert became suspicious. I don't think Romero could have detected it any earlier."

Juanita shrugged. "Still, he feels responsible. He's the manager."

"Well, in hindsight, it's always easier," Janice said. "I bet from now on everybody will be more careful, including Robert. Perhaps that'll get him to stay around more instead of hobnobbing all over the universe."

Juanita pursed her lips. "That will be the day."

"Tell Romero not to worry." Janice took another sip of wine. "They'll figure it out. Yes, it's an unpleasant situation, but it's nobody's fault, except the culprit's. That's what worries me the most. I still hope it's someone from outside and not a member of the staff."

"I hope so, too," Juanita said, thoughtfully.

Chapter 18

"Hi, Matt, want to try a piece? I just made a new kind of pie. I need a guinea pig." Janice pushed the raspberry custard pie toward her son.

"Oh? Sure." Matthew gave a weak smile.

Janice was surprised at her son's subdued reaction. "Wow. Where's your usual enthusiasm when it comes to dessert? You're not feeling well?"

Matthew looked troubled. "I need to talk to you." He put a finger in his mouth and chewed on a cuticle. Janice took his hand in hers and noticed that his nails had been bitten. He used to do this as a boy when he was nervous or worried. Something must be really bothering him.

"What's wrong?" *Are there tears in his eyes?* "What's the matter, honey?"

"It's about Marcia." Matthew's voice trembled.

"What about her? I thought you guys broke up?"

"Yes, we did." Another sigh. "Mom, she claims she's pregnant and that I'm most likely the father."

Janice felt a jolt in her stomach. "What?"

Matthew nodded. "Yeah. I'm not sure what to think."

"Well, wait a minute. She's not on birth control? Didn't you use protection?" Janice glared at Matthew.

"Sure. I always used condoms, but … one time it broke. Marcia claimed it wasn't a dangerous time. She didn't seem worried at all."

Janice's head was spinning. "Then how come she claims it's yours? Didn't you say she had other boyfriends as well?"

"Yep. That's why I broke up with her."

"But you broke up with her quite some time ago. If she got pregnant while being with you, she must have known for weeks. Why didn't she say anything earlier?"

"She told me a while ago. I just didn't have the courage to tell anybody."

"Oh, Matthew, you shouldn't hide something like this. You know you can always talk to me about anything." Janice put her arm around her son.

"I know." Matthew brushed through his dark, curly hair, then rubbed his brow. "I told her I wanted a paternity test."

"Yes, definitely. You know this whole thing sounds fishy to me. She slept around and now she picks you as the father, a son from a well-to-do family. How convenient."

"I know. I thought the same. But, Mom, what if it's true? What am I going to do? I know I'd have to take responsibility for the child. But I don't want to marry her. I don't love her anymore."

"Of course you don't have to marry her. And yes, you would need to take responsibility. You know we'll stand by you if that happens. But I'm not convinced she's telling the truth. You know her mother is in the same women's volunteer club as I am. Isn't it odd that she didn't say anything?"

Matthew shrugged. "I don't think she told her mother."

"How far along would she be?"

"About two months, I guess. A little more. That's when we were last together. If I'm the dad, I mean."

"You need to contact Marcia immediately and insist on the paternity test. We need to know."

Matthew nodded. "Yes, I'll call her today. I found information on paternity tests that can be done as early as ten weeks into the pregnancy, which would be about now. It's not a difficult test. I've mentioned it several times, but she's evasive."

"That's probably because she may be lying. Tell her that if she doesn't comply, we'll talk to her mother."

"Okay. But please, Mom, don't tell Dad yet."

"Matthew, this is important. Your father needs to know."

"Yes, I need to tell him eventually. But he'll just kill me or find another reason to think I'm a failure."

"Matthew, that's total nonsense. He does not think you're a failure. Yeah, he can be somewhat rough sometimes. Just the other day, though, he told me that you're doing a great job developing a plan for upgrading the cellar."

Matthew gave a quick smile. "Thanks. I need to get back to work." He walked toward the door.

"No pie?" Janice asked.

Matthew turned around. "I'm not really hungry."

"Take some with you for later."

"Oh, all right."

Janice went into the kitchen, cut a large piece, and put it into a Tupperware dish.

"Thanks, Mom." Matthew gave her a hug and took the dish. "It looks yummy. I'll have it for dessert … or dinner." He chuckled. "It's big enough for a whole meal."

"Enjoy." Janice kissed him. "And, please, don't worry too much. Call Marcia right away and get it over with. And remember, we're on your side. Tell me as soon as you hear from her. Okay?"

"Yes, thanks. I feel better now having told you." Matthew gave his mother a hug, then opened the door.

"Love you, Matt."

"Love you, too, Mom."

Janice watched as he walked across the lawn to his house. "Oh, God." She went back inside. "That's all we need. As if there wasn't enough turmoil already."

She poured a glass of water and drank it slowly, wondering if she should tell Robert. She felt the need to talk to someone, but she had promised Matt to let *him* tell his dad. Should she call Elizabeth, Marcia's mother? They knew each other from the women's club, and they had become friends mainly because their children had dated. They didn't have much in common. Elizabeth didn't seem to have many interests aside from being a wife and mother. She wasn't into reading, music or anything artistic, things that Janice enjoyed. Elizabeth, however, was kind and likable.

Janice shook her head. She needed to let Matthew take the initiative first and get Marcia to agree to a paternity test.

"What a mess." Janice groaned. She went to the window and looked outside. On the horizon, a few dark clouds had gathered. A gusty wind blew through the azaleas in the corner of the patio. She hoped it wouldn't rain. The grapes were almost fully ripe, and rain could easily damage the fruit. In the distance, sirens blared.

Now, she understood Matthew's gloomy mood the past few weeks. She had associated it with the tension between him and his father. Obviously, that wasn't the only reason. She wished though that Robert wouldn't be so hard on Matthew. The boy tried so hard to please his father. She knew he wasn't as confident and experienced yet as Nicholas was. Matthew had always been the slower of the two all through childhood. Studying had come easy to Nicholas whereas Matthew had struggled in school but had blossomed in college and he was a hard worker. So Robert should focus on his strengths more and not on his weaknesses. The more he badgered him, the less confident their son became. It was a bad situation.

Janice continued to watch the ominous-looking clouds in the sky. What was going on in her family? Someone was stealing and selling wine from the estate and Robert and Matthew were at each other's throat all the time.

Chapter 19

"You didn't tell me you got a bunch of criminals as phony agents. He doesn't use agents for his sales here."

"You never mentioned it."

"Yes, I did."

"Look, it's the only way I can recoup some of the money you owe me. I hired a few of my friends, promised them a cut, had them use fake names and non-traceable cell phones. They contacted the outfits that didn't know the Segantino label very well. They ordered, paid me, and it worked."

"It didn't work. He found out. One of the merchants called your so-called agent to order more wine and couldn't get a hold of him. So, he called Robert. Now, he's going to get the police involved."

"Don't worry. They can't trace anything. Nothing leads back to me … or to you. Besides, the bottles brought me a decent amount. Works for you, too. You owe me less."

"What are we doing now? What about the rest of the bottles? What if they find them?"

"They won't find them. Didn't you say the shed isn't used anymore? We'll just leave the bottles there for now."

"No, it's not used right now, but it's too dangerous to leave them there. If the authorities get involved, they may search the whole place. We can't keep them in the shed any longer."

"Don't worry. I'll find a way to move the bottles off the property. Just give me a day or two. I know of a place we can store them. Now we lay low for a while until this whole thing blows over."

"It won't blow over. I can't do it anymore. It just isn't right."

"Jesus, dude. You work your butt off for a lousy salary. You have no real authority. You're at his beck and call."

"I can't betray him like this."

"Then how are you going to pay me? I'm giving you a real opportunity here. Just a few more times and we're even. I won't insist on the whole amount you owe me."

"I'll pay you. Just give me some time."

"How much? It's been months now."

"You know it's been a tough year."

"How do you think I feel? No job. No future. Wife gone. No contact with the kids. And it's all because of that bastard. All I want is some justice."

"I'll pay you some other way, but I won't do this anymore."

"Well, dude, you should've thought of that before. You're in too far. If it came out now, you'd be in deep shit."

"Is this a threat? Are you now into blackmail as well?"

"Just a reality check."

"You bastard."

"Come on, don't be like this. It'll all work out."

At home, a few hours later, he watched the sun set behind a bank of gray clouds. What had he done? He'd ruined everything, got himself involved with a bunch of criminals. All he had wanted was a little more money to pay off some debts. Instead, he got tangled in a web of lies. He had betrayed family and friends and everybody who loved and trusted him. And for what?

He got up with a heavy heart, giving the darkening sky one last glance. He needed to confess. But that would destroy his life. He couldn't do it. He was too far into this mess. Tears filled his eyes, tears of anguish, an anguish and despair he couldn't share with anyone.

Chapter 20

"Hey, Mark, how are you?" Robert waved at his neighbor who came walking up the path to his home.

"Great, thanks, and yourself?" Mark Llewellyn asked.

"Busy, as always." Robert smiled.

"Listen, you wouldn't happen to have some temporary storage space for wine bottles?" Mark asked. "One of our facilities needs a makeover and I'm afraid it'll take longer than anticipated. We're getting ready to pick our Pinot Noir. And we need some space for the few artisan wines from last harvest. It's about two hundred bottles. I'd pay you rent of course."

Robert motioned him to sit on one of the chairs on the patio. "We have an old shed we don't use anymore. It's well insulated and we used to store wine there. You don't have to pay anything. The building is empty and unlocked. Check it out and let me know. You know where it is? Near my manager's home."

"Yes, I think I know which one you're talking about. That would be great. We won't need it for more than a month, tops."

"No problem. As I said, it's not locked, but once you move the bottles inside, use a padlock and make sure you lock up. We've had some strange things happening."

"Oh, really?" Mark, a short and skinny man with dark hair and receding hairline, gave Robert a questioning look.

"Yeah, I don't know what's going on, but we're missing some cases of wine, among other things." Robert didn't want to go into any details, since he wasn't sure yet what was happening.

"Gee, that's rough," Mark said. "Hope you'll sort it out."

"Yeah, I hope so, too. Anyway, go right ahead, and you can have the place as long as necessary. We really don't need it anymore. We have that new storage facility that should last us a while."

"Thanks, I really appreciate it." Mark gave a quick smile.

"Would you like some coffee?" Robert asked. "I was just getting ready to have one myself."

"Sure, that would be great."

Robert got up and went into the kitchen. He pressed the button on the espresso machine and filled two cups with coffee. He brought them outside and the two men began to talk shop, discussing the upcoming harvest.

"I just hope this drought is going to be over one of these days … or years." Mark harrumphed. "The dry weather is good for the grapes, but the excessive heat is a threat to my Pinot. If this global warming thing keeps getting worse, I'll have to switch to another varietal or even consider a different crop."

"It couldn't be that bad, could it?" Robert said. "At least I hope not."

"Well, I hate to sound negative or be a doomsayer, but this climate change will eventually bite us all in the ass … unless we come up with a solution."

Robert nodded. "Yeah, it's a complex problem, and I don't know the solution either. So far, we've done really well with our wine, but, as you say, who knows what the future holds."

Mark chuckled. "I told my wife we may have to move north. Canada may be the future wine country. 'No way. Too cold,' she says."

Robert laughed. "It would be easier to move west. Cambria may be next. It already has some great vineyards."

"True," Mark got up. "Well, thanks for the coffee and thanks for letting me use your place. Much appreciated."

"No problem. Let me know if you need help with moving the wine." Robert got up as well and carried the empty cups into the kitchen.

A couple of hours later, Mark was back. "Say, you said the place was open. But there's already a padlock on it and it's locked."

Robert stared at him. "That's odd. I'll have to find out who locked it. Sorry, I hope you didn't drag your wine over there already."

"Oh, no, I just wanted to check it out."

"Okay, listen I'll figure out what's going on, and I'll let you know when I find out who has the key to the lock."

"No problem," Mark said. "Just give me a call when it's ready."

Robert walked into the Accounting Department looking for Ken. Adam sat in front of the computer, doing data entry, Robert assumed. He still didn't feel comfortable, having his enemy's nephew on the estate, but Adam was a hard worker, and everybody liked him.

"Ken, do you know anything about the old wine storage shed, you know the one behind Romero's place? It used to be unlocked, but now there is a padlock on the door."

Ken's eyes widened. "No, no idea. I haven't seen that place in a while. Isn't it empty? We're not using it anymore, right?"

"Yes, that's why I'm surprised it's locked. Mark from the Llewellyn estate needs a temporary storage space for some wine. We need to open the place. Anyway, if you hear anything about a key to the lock, let me know."

"Sure, I will. Perhaps Romero knows something."

"Yeah, where is he anyway? Oh, yes, he went to San Luis Obispo with some paperwork. I'll ask him later. If we can't find the key, we'll have to break open the padlock."

Ken nodded, then looked down at his papers.

Robert glanced at Adam, who had watched them as they talked. Avoiding Robert's eyes, Adam went back to entering data.

He is definitely trying to hide something.

After leaving the office, Robert called Matthew on his cell phone. He didn't know anything about the locked building either. Neither did the rest of the family nor the workers. Robert decided to wait until Romero got home. He was the most likely one to know something about it.

In the evening, Robert called Romero's house. Juanita answered and told him Romero should be home any minute. Robert asked her if she knew anything about the padlock on the storage shed behind their home.

"No, Mr. Segantino," she said. "Maybe Romero does."

"Yes. Well, have him call me when he gets home."

About half an hour later, Romero called. "No, I have no idea who put the lock on. I hardly ever pay attention to the shed. And I don't have the key." He sounded concerned.

"That's odd," Robert said. "I asked everybody who could have locked it, and nobody knew anything."

Romero cleared his throat. "That *is* odd. What are we going to do?"

"Well, tomorrow, we'll have to break the lock open." Robert explained about his friend wanting to store some bottles of wine."

No answer. "Are you still there?" Robert asked.

"Yes. Are you sure the shed is still suited for storing wine?" Romero said in a low voice. "It hasn't been used in a while."

"Oh, it should be all right. It's well insulated, and Mark wouldn't need it for very long."

"Okay," Romero said. "Want me to do anything?"

"No, don't worry. Tomorrow is early enough. No rush."

"Okay, have a good evening."

The somberness of Romero's tone touched Robert. "Are you all right, my friend? Did everything go okay at City Hall?"

"Yes, no problem, everything went smoothly."

"Is Nora okay?"

Romero hesitated. "More or less."

"Listen, have a good night. Talk to you tomorrow."

They hung up and Robert put the phone down and looked out the window. From his living room, he had a great view of the setting sun. Janice came into the room.

"Did you get a hold of Romero?" she asked.

"Yes, he doesn't know anything about it either. We'll just have to break open the lock. It's just odd." He paused. "I feel bad for Romero. He sounded kind of down. I think he's worried again about Nora."

Janice sat down next to him and hugged him briefly. "I'll go and visit with Juanita again tomorrow. See if they need any help," she said.

"Thanks, yes, that's a good idea." Robert smiled.

Chapter 21

Sirens woke Nicholas in the middle of the night. He got out of bed and stared through the window, then hurried downstairs. Sofia had woken up as well and followed him. They stepped out on the patio and saw a huge blaze in the direction of Robert's estate. Nicholas ran inside and grabbed the phone, trying to call his father, but Robert didn't answer his cell phone. He then called the landline, and his mother answered, telling him she didn't know what was going on, but his dad had left to check the source of the fire. It looked like the blaze was close to the edge of the property, near Romero's house.

Nicholas put down the phone. "I got to go. Are you going to be okay by yourself here?"

"Sure, but call me as soon as you know what's going on," Sofia said.

"Of course." Nicholas rushed upstairs, and Sofia followed him. In the bedroom, he pulled on his pants and a T-shirt, then stepped into the hall. He paused to glance into the nursery where Henry was deep asleep.

Julietta opened the door of her bedroom and stared at them with eyes still full of sleep. "What's going on?"

Sofia began to tell her while Nicholas grabbed the car keys and rushed outside.

It smelled of fire and gasoline. To make matters worse, a dry wind kicked up. *Please let it not be one of our places.* Nicholas's heart pounded as he raced his car up the hill past his father's house toward the edge of the estate. Was it Romero's place? There were flames shooting out from behind the manager's home. Nicholas parked at the side of the road. He couldn't see much at first because the view was blocked by fire engines and police cars.

As he moved closer, a terrifying scene unfolded. While the firemen were trying to extinguish the flames shooting out of what looked like the old wine storage shed, Romero, a hose in his hands, was spraying water on the grass and bushes between the burning building and his home.

"Stand back. Get back," one of the firefighters yelled at Romero. "We'll take care of this." One of the men rushed toward him. Then a piece of the burning roof dropped and hit Romero. He tried to shake it off, but to the horror of everyone, he burst into flames. Another piece of the roof struck him, and he fell to the ground. Firefighters rushed toward him, pulled away the pieces of roof, and covered Romero with a cloth, trying to extinguish the flames.

Nicholas stared at the scene, uncomprehending. His father held Juanita, who was screaming. Medical personnel attended to Romero. They lifted him on a gurney and carried him over to the emergency vehicle. Robert and Juanita followed. Before climbing into the ambulance, Juanita turned around. "Nora?" she called.

"I'll get her," Janice rushed toward the door, where Nora, dressed in pajamas and holding a robe in her hand, appeared in her wheelchair. She was in tears. Janice hugged her, put the robe around the girl's shoulders, then pushed the chair over to the van. Robert helped her get Nora secured with a seatbelt and the wheelchair into the back. They got into the car and Janice drove away, following the ambulance.

"Oh my God," Nicholas gasped and looked around frantically. He felt sick to his stomach and was afraid he was going to throw up. He took deep breaths until he felt less nauseated, then walked over to his grandfather, who was standing next to one of the firefighters. "What happened?"

Martin's face was pale. He put his arm around Nicholas. "This is just horrible."

"I hope Romero is going to be okay," Nicholas said. "It looked really bad." His eyes burned, he squeezed them shut.

"I know." Martin's voice shook.

"What caused the fire?" Nicholas asked. "Why was the shed burning?"

Martin lifted a shoulder. "I don't know."

"I heard something like gunshots." Nicholas stared at the smoldering building.

Martin nodded. "I did, too. Something was in the shed. It wasn't empty."

Gloom settled over the Segantino estate. In the afternoon, Robert had called and told the rest of the family that Romero had succumbed to his injuries and died. His wife and daughter were devastated. Janice stayed with them until Juanita's sister who lived nearby came to support them.

Everybody was in shock. Matthew, Nicholas, Sofia, and Julietta were with Martin and Maria. Little Henry, peacefully oblivious to all the torment, was asleep in his crib in Maria and Martin's bedroom.

Later that afternoon, Janice joined them. She looked exhausted with circles under red-rimmed eyes. "Here's what I learned," she said.

"Juanita had woken up in the middle of the night and noticed that Romero wasn't in bed, so she went to check on him. He was outside, walking around the shed. He told her that he heard something and wanted to check. Juanita noticed a faint smell of gasoline and asked Romero about it. He shrugged and said he had smelled it, too, but didn't see anything. He told her to go back to bed. He would be right there as well, he just wanted to check around the house to make sure everything was all right." Janice paused. "Can I have some water? My mouth is parched."

Maria went into the kitchen and brought her a glass of water. "Here you go, honey."

"Thanks." Janice took a few sips and put the glass down.

"Anyway, Juanita went back to lie down. Just as she was about to doze off, she smelled something like burning wood and, again, gasoline. She got back up and saw Romero outside, pulling the hose toward the shed, which to her shock was engulfed in flames. He told her to call the fire department. When she came outside, she heard popping sounds coming from the burning shed. Romero was frantically spraying the grass between their house and the shed. She screamed for him not to get too close. That's when the fire engines arrived."

The rest of the family members sat in silence, stunned at what Janice had told them.

Finally, Nicholas looked around at the shocked faces. "Why was the shed burning? What was in it? Grandpa, you heard the popping noises, too?"

Martin nodded. "It sounded like bottles exploding."

"Bottles?" Sofia stared at him.

"Wine bottles?" Nicholas said. "The missing bottles?"

"I'm afraid that's possible." Martin brushed through his white hair. "We'll find out more tomorrow. They're going to investigate the cause of the fire?"

"It smelled of gasoline," Sofia said. "Does that mean it was set deliberately?"

"Looks like it," Martin said.

"But why?" Nicholas asked. "Why would someone do that?"

Martin shrugged. "If it turns out the bottles in there were the missing Cabs and whoever stole and hid them there knew that the shed was going to be opened, perhaps they tried to destroy the evidence?"

"Jesus. Who knew, though?" Sofia looked around.

"More or less everybody," Martin said, "after Robert tried to find the person who had the key to unlock the padlock."

More stunned silence.

Maria sighed deeply. "Whatever way you look at it, it's a terrible catastrophe. Poor Romero and poor Juanita and Nora. As if the family didn't have enough to worry about what with Nora's illness. How could this happen on our estate?" Her voice broke. Martin put his arm around his wife.

"Oh, God." Matthew covered his face and started to cry. Nicholas watched him concerned. Tears welled in his eyes as he thought back to the terrible scene of Romero engulfed in flames.

In the evening, Nicholas came home just as Sofia and Julietta were putting Henry to bed. He kissed the little boy good night and went into the living room where Sofia poured them each a glass of wine.

"I think we could use something relaxing," she said with a sigh.

Nicholas took a sip of wine. "Dad told me, the authorities are going to send someone with a so-called arson-sniffing dog."

"Arson-sniffing dog?" Julietta asked stunned. "Never even heard of such a thing."

"Neither had I," Nicholas said. "Not sure how it works, but they're coming tomorrow."

"My God. How certain are they that it could be arson?" Sofia asked.

"Pretty certain, or they wouldn't bring in the dog," Nicholas said. "I think they just want to double-check."

"But who could do something like this?" Sofia asked in a low voice.

"No idea," Nicholas said. "But if it's arson, then the peace of our estate is gone." He rubbed his eyes.

"Yes, that's true," Sofia said, her voice shaking.

"And what's even worse, it could've been one of us," Nicholas said. "I mean an employee ... or ... and I don't even want to think about it, a member of the family."

Sofia shook her head energetically. "No way, that's just not possible." She stared at Nicholas and Julietta with an expression of pain in her eyes.

"I hope not either," Nicholas murmured. "Well, tomorrow, we may know more."

Chapter 22

The following day, a team of investigators arrived. One of them was David Lauer, a federal prosecutor. According to Walt Smith, the sheriff, Lauer was an expert on arson and crimes involving wine. He would be leading the investigation. Romero's death added possible manslaughter charges to whatever case they came up with.

Robert watched as a tall, slim man with a crew cut and piercing gray eyes, most likely in his forties, holding a dog on the leash, was walking slowly around the area of the shed and the home of the Guerrero family. He approached the man and the two shook hands. David Lauer explained that Buster, a German Shepherd, was an arson dog, trained to detect accelerants.

Up till then, the site of the fire had been cordoned off. Now, Lauer and one other man and the dog entered the shed. Robert, Janice, Matthew, Nicholas, Sofia and a few of the workers waited outside. The mood was dark and gloomy.

A few sharp barks sounded from inside. Robert and the others glanced at each other, then at the burnt building. A few moments later, the men came back out, carrying a bundle of charred, black rags. Buster acted excited, barking and wagging his tail. Lauer gave the dog a treat. Then he turned to the people.

"I need all of you to be available for questioning. Don't leave the property, until I or my men have talked to you, okay?" He scanned the people with his penetrating eyes. "And don't go inside the building. It's a crime scene now, and besides, it's dangerous. The rest of the roof can collapse anytime."

"Of course, we'll all be available," Robert said. He had been able to catch a glimpse of the inside of the shed through the open door when the men and the dog entered. He was shocked to detect charred shrink-wrapped boxes used to store wine bottles. There was a pile of shattered bottles. It smelled of charred wood, smoke, and, yes, wine. What was wine doing in the shed? It was supposed to be empty. Was this the wine they had missed for months, the stolen wine? Who had put the bottles into the shed?

Lauer motioned him to step aside. Out of earshot of the other people, he faced him. "Definitely arson. The job must have been done by an amateur, but it was partly effective." He pointed at the heap of rags that the other men of the team put into plastic containers.

Later, in Robert's office, Janice, Robert, and David Lauer were discussing the situation.

"This is just terrible," Robert muttered. "Who would do something like this?" Then he remembered the anonymous letters he had received a few months ago. They had stopped in the meantime.

"The letters?" Janice said, echoing Robert's thoughts. "Didn't you give them to the sheriff?"

"I was going to, but I never got around to it. And they stopped, so I forgot about them, but now?"

"What letters?" Lauer asked.

Robert told him about a few anonymous letters he had received several months before. He showed him the last one he had kept. Lauer perused it, then looked up. "Have you received any more?"

"No, and that's why I didn't pursue it any further."

"Any suspicions?" Lauer asked.

"The only person that comes to mind is this crazy woman, a Mrs. Selby. We call her the Water Queen. She and a few of her friends protest in front of vineyards and wineries, claiming we're raping the land, wasting water, and poisoning people with alcohol. She's clearly unstable, but I've always considered her harmless."

"Honey, you should've reported the letters," Janice said.

"I know," Robert said. "Matt gave me a hard time about it, too." He hesitated. "Do you really think she could've done all this?" He motioned with his hand in the direction of the burnt shed.

"I actually doubt it," Janice said. "I mean stealing wine, selling it, and burning down a shed? I don't think she'd steal or sell wine. She's a member of an anti-alcohol organization after all."

"Well, we'll look into it, of course. And if you get any more letters, let me know right away. Okay?" Lauer measured Robert with a stern look.

Robert nodded. "Of course."

"What about the person who died?" Lauer continued. "How was he involved in your business? I know he was the manager. How well do you know him?" Lauer asked.

"Very well. We have been friends for many years and our two families are close."

"You don't think he could've had anything to do with the wine theft?" Lauer gave him and Janice a questioning look. Janice shook her head.

"No way," Robert said. "Absolutely not."

"I'm just curious. The wine was stored in a shed close to his home. Wouldn't he have seen if anybody had hidden bottles of wine in there? I mean whoever put the bottles into the shed would've had to go in and out. And the Guerreros wouldn't have noticed?"

"Not necessarily," Janice said.

"No," Robert repeated. "As you saw, the door to the shed is on the side facing away from Romero's home. Anybody could've gone in and out without him noticing it. Also, there was brush between his home and the shed, which the fire burnt away. Nobody paid attention to that old building. And couldn't whoever hid the wine have done it at night or at a time the family wasn't outside watching?"

"They could have," Lauer acknowledged.

"You don't seriously think Romero had anything to do with this? I mean he was the one who saw the fire and called the fire department. He tried to extinguish it. If he wanted to hide the bottles, he could've let the shed burn down. No, Inspector, you're barking up the wrong tree."

Lauer shrugged. "What puzzles me is the fact that he himself burned so fast. Witnesses told me that he literally burst into flames. We checked his clothes. The bottoms of his pant legs were soaked in gasoline. Why?"

Robert frowned and paused. "The only thing I can think of is that whoever set the fire spilled gasoline on the grass around the shed as well as inside," Robert said. "When Romero went to check, he may have unknowingly dragged his pant legs through the gasoline."

Lauer gave a quick nod. "It's possible."

After Lauer had left, Robert put his head on his hands. "What a calamity. I still can't believe it. And poor Romero." His voice broke. He took a deep breath and a sob escaped him. He felt Janice's hand on his back and lifted his head.

"I know it's terrible," Janice said. "We'll have to take care of Juanita and Nora. This is such a blow to them."

"Where are they now?" Robert asked, wiping a tear from his face.

Janice gave him a quick hug. "They're staying with Juanita's sister and family in San Luis Obispo. I'll check on them later."

"Lauer said he was going to question everybody on the estate, including the family." Robert shrugged. "I guess that's normal procedure."

Chapter 23

Matthew, his face red and scrunched, burst into Sofia and Nicholas's home.

"Hey, Matt, what's the matter with you?" Nicholas stared at his brother. "You're all hot and bothered."

Nicholas and Sofia had just finished their lunch. Sofia was sitting on the sofa, holding Henry and getting him ready for his nap.

"You'd be hot and bothered, too, if you experienced what I had to go through just now," Matthew said.

"Come on, bro, get it out or you'll pop a vein."

"Fucking asshole." Matthew plopped himself down on the sofa, then put his hand over his mouth. "Sorry, shouldn't curse like that in front of little Henry." His facial expression changed from angry to loving, as he gently touched the baby's head. Henry's face broke into a smile and he waved his arms, unperturbed by his uncle's upheaval.

"I'll put him down for his nap. You two can talk it out." Sofia patted Matthew on the shoulder. She carried Henry into the nursery.

"Want some coffee?" Nicholas asked Matthew.

"No, I'm keyed up enough as it is. But get some for yourself." Matthew got up and walked to the window. Nicholas went into the kitchen and poured himself a cup of espresso. When he came back, he sat on the sofa. "Sit down and relax."

Matthew, however, remained standing, then began to pace. "So, you know, we all get questioned by Lauer. I understand. He asks me if I had any money problems, if I sold the stolen wine illegally. I'm getting pissed, but I still kind of get it that probably everybody gets asked that."

"Okay, so what's so upsetting?" Nicholas tried to understand his brother's fury.

"Well, then he told me he heard I had a possible paternity suit hanging over my head. Which may cost me a lot of money, so, perhaps I was looking for ways to increase my bottom-line. Bottom-line? The arrogant son of a … And how does he know about the paternity business?" Matthew sat down again.

Nicholas stared at his brother. "Paternity what? What are you talking about?"

Matthew hesitated, then sat down, leaned forward, propped his elbows on his knees, and covered his face with his hands. "I may have fathered a child," he mumbled.

"What? Now, you lost me," Nicholas said. "I assume it's Marcia you're talking about. Is she pregnant? You broke up a while ago. I don't get it. And why didn't you tell us?"

Matthew waved his hand dismissively. "I would've told you once I knew myself what's really going on. I didn't want Dad to know before it was certain one way or the other. So, please don't tell him. And, to be honest, I was ashamed. I mean who gets pregnant by accident in the twenty-first century?"

"Okay, but what does this have to do with stealing wine?"

"Exactly, that's what I told stupid Lauer, too. But anyway, I guess I should start from the beginning."

Sofia came into the room, carrying a cup of espresso. She sat next to Nicholas. "No coffee for you, Matt?"

Matthew shook his head.

Nicholas snorted. "He doesn't need coffee. He's already keyed up beyond repair."

Another sigh from Matthew. "Anyway, here's what happened." He told Nicholas and Sofia about Marcia claiming she was pregnant and that it was his. He asked her to do a paternity test, one of those you can do before the baby is born. She agreed, but then never got back to him. He was still waiting to hear from her.

"Oh, my God." Sofia said. "What would you do if the baby was yours?"

Matthew shrugged. "Pay up I guess, child support. I'm not going to marry her, that's for sure. We don't love each other. She was seeing other guys on the side. But, of course, I'd need to support the child."

"Okay. We'll talk about this later," Nicholas said. "But why would Lauer think you stole the wine?"

"To sell it and make extra money, of course. And since they discovered that the stolen wine was stored at the shed, he thinks I might have burned it down to destroy the evidence. They did find bottles that were still intact after the fire and they are the Cabs that went missing."

Nicholas got up, walked over to his brother, put his hand on his shoulder, and gave him an encouraging squeeze. "Matt, even if it was true about the paternity case and that you needed money, you're only one of many people on this estate who could profit from extra cash. I'm sure Lauer will question everybody. We could be suspects, too. We probably are. Including Dad. So just calm down, be honest, and cooperate. They'll find the guilty party. I know you didn't do it."

"Then why did he question me first?" Matthew said in a low voice.

"How do you know you were first? He may have questioned some of the staff, too." Nicholas said.

Sofia took a sip of coffee. "Matthew, if you really were going to be a father, you know we'll help you. The family will support you."

Matthew nodded. "Thanks. I still think Marcia's wrong, but I need to get this checked. I need to talk to her again. She needs to do that test. Anyway, guys, I'm sorry for just barging in and spreading my anger."

"It's okay, Matt. We understand," Sofia said. "If it was your child, would you want to be involved at all, you know, in his or her upbringing?"

Matthew lifted his hands, then let them fall on his knees. "I don't know. It seems all so unreal. But I guess if it really was my child … well, yes, I'd like to be involved. I mean it's not the baby's fault … oh, God, what have I gotten myself into?" He covered his face with his hands for a moment, then looked up. "Anyway, I need to go. I haven't done a stitch of work today because of all this upset." Matthew got up, patted Nicholas on the back, kissed Sofia's cheek, and left.

Nicholas followed his brother to the door and watched him walk away. "He looks like he carries the world on his back," he said to Sofia.

"What a mess. I hope this paternity thing is going to be settled soon. Poor Matt." Sofia glanced at Nicholas, opened her mouth, then closed it again.

"What?" Nicholas asked.

"Oh, it's impossible. Do you think it could be true?"

"Which?" Nicholas gave a quick sharp laugh that didn't sound happy. "His being a dad or him having stolen the wine and burned down the shed?"

"You don't really believe he could've done that." Sofia stared at him.

Nicholas exhaled deeply. "Not really. Then again, he's been acting strange lately. And he has some very mixed feelings toward Dad. Also, he seems to always need more money. He says it's for the estate. That's what I always thought. But what if …. No, I don't even want to go there."

He looked at Sofia. She stared at him but didn't say anything.

Chapter 24

"Any news?" Robert eyed David Lauer sharply. The two sat in Robert's home office.

"Some, yes." Lauer gave a quick smile when Janice brought in two cups of coffee. "Thank you, ma'am."

"Anyway, we found the person who wrote the letters." Lauer looked from Janice to Robert. "You were right with your suspicion. It was Mrs. Selby."

"I knew it, damn it. That crazy woman." Robert inhaled sharply. "But did she do the rest?"

Lauer shook his head. "No, she clearly wasn't involved in the wine theft and sale, and she has a solid alibi for the night the shed burned. Mrs. Selby strikes me as emotionally and mentally unstable, but I doubt she has the capacity to organize the kind of theft and sale that's taking place. I also don't think she's that vindictive or violent. She'll be charged with harassment and we'll put a restraining order on her to keep her away from your estate and your family. You most likely won't have to deal with her anymore."

"So, what about the rest, the wine theft and so on?" Robert asked.

"Nothing definite yet, but we're looking at everything."

"I need to leave," Janice said. "You can fill me in later."

"Okay, see you later," Robert said.

Lauer got up and nodded a farewell to Janice. He was always polite and gentlemanly in an old-fashioned way. The sheriff and other people familiar with Lauer had told Robert, however, that he was ruthless and unswerving in his pursuit of criminals. And Robert saw it in his stern and penetrating gray eyes.

After Janice had left, Lauer cleared his throat. "One thing I did notice. A few people among your staff and your family seem to be short of cash and could probably profit from some extra money."

"Oh? Who?" Robert asked.

"Ken Miller, your accountant, for instance, has been complaining about lack of money, according to some witnesses. His wife seems to be somewhat of a spendthrift. He, too, might need some extra cash."

"Ken?" Robert waved his hand in a dismissive gesture. "I don't think so. He asked me for a raise a year ago, and I granted it. If he needed money, he'd tell me. He's a loyal and long-term employee. No, I don't think he has anything to do with it." He paused, then continued, his voice tense. "The sooner this is cleared up, the sooner we can go on with our lives. This is a terrible thing hanging over the whole estate, my family and employees. We need to find the answer."

"We're doing our best, believe me," Lauer continued. He sat up straight. "There's a death involved, which makes our investigation even more critical."

"What about Adam Winter?" Robert asked. "As I told you his uncle is a criminal and he must hate me. I was instrumental in his getting fired. What if he asked his nephew to steal from me, just out of spite, maybe?"

"But didn't the wine begin to disappear before he was hired?" Lauer asked.

"Well ... we first discovered it in July, which was after Adam began to work here. But it could've started before. We don't really know."

"Okay. So, Adam, too, is a possible suspect. We'll look into his background as well." Lauer faced him with slightly narrowed eyes. "One of the things we need to do is check people's financial transactions, you know bank statements, looking for unusual amounts deposited or withdrawn. That's just common procedure. That would help us narrow down possible suspects."

Robert nodded.

"And I have to remind you that members of your family are among the suspects as well. Both of your sons could have a motive. They have some financial burdens, where some extra money could've helped."

Robert knitted his brows. "What do you mean?"

"Well, for instance, your older son, Nicholas, and his wife have a pretty steep mortgage that seems to worry them. At least, that was my impression."

"Yes, but they're doing all right. And even if they'd run into problems, I as well as my father would help them out. Nicholas is not the kind of person who would resort to being a small-time thief. And there's no way he would sell our wine illegally, and he certainly wouldn't burn down a building." Robert talked himself into anger. "What are you implying?"

Lauer held up his hand. "I'm not implying anything. First of all, we don't know yet if the wine was stolen and sold by the same person. There could be two people involved, or more. And also we don't know if that person or those people burnt down the shed. It looks that way, but it's by no means certain."

"What about my other son? Matthew doesn't have any money problems I know of," Robert said.

"He has a possible paternity suit looming over him," Lauer said.

"What? What are you talking about?" Robert stared at him.

"You didn't know about it?" Lauer gave him a penetrating look.

Robert jumped up from his chair, almost knocking it over. "I had no idea. I'm sorry. I'm totally confused. Listen, I need to go. I need to talk to my family. Obviously, I don't know the first thing about them. But even if that's true, about Matthew and … he'd never do anything like this." Robert's heart was racing. *Or would he?*

"Well, you may not be the most impartial judge when it comes to your family. I understand. Again, these are all just conjectures. The whole thing is very murky and we're at the beginning of our investigation."

"Okay, can we talk later? I really need to go."

"Certainly. It's late anyway. I'll see you tomorrow." Lauer got up gave a quick smile, then left.

Robert stared at Lauer leaving without really seeing him. "Matthew? What the heck…?" He grabbed his cell phone and tried to call Matthew but only got his voicemail. "Damn him." He tossed his phone into his pocket and hurried toward Matthew's house, but his son wasn't home.

Robert took a deep breath, trying to calm down, and walked home. He yanked the door open and rushed inside, almost bumping into Janice.

"Did you know about Matthew's paternity suit?" he yelled at his wife. "What the hell is going on, and why didn't I know about it?"

"Calm down." Janice held up her hands. "I just found out a couple of days ago myself, and he asked me not to tell you. He wanted to do it himself. Besides, there isn't a paternity suit yet. It's just that Marcia claims she's pregnant and that Matt might be the father."

"And that's not important enough to let me know?" Robert yelled at the top of his voice. "I had to find out from David Lauer, for God's sake. How embarrassing."

"Is this all you care about? How not knowing your own family makes you look?" Janice faced him. "If you paid a little more attention to the people around you instead of to your business—"

"Oh, for God's sake." Robert rushed out of the room and the house and slammed the door. Deep down, he knew though that his wife was right. He looked around at his estate, the fields of grapes, full of ripening fruit, his own Tuscan style home, the thin strip of purple on the horizon, reflection of the sun that had set a few hours ago. And yet, despite all that beauty, of all he had achieved, he felt a growing emptiness in his heart.

He walked along fields of grapes toward his parents' home. When he arrived at their house, there was no light shining through the windows. He glanced at his watch. It was past ten o'clock. He knew that his parents went to bed fairly early. Not wanting to wake them up, he sat down on one of the garden chairs on their patio.

Robert glanced at the dark fields around him. The grapevines along the hill on the left rustled lightly in the evening breeze. He propped his elbows on his knees and covered his face with his hands. He took deep breaths to calm his racing heart, then looked up again.

He tried to bring some order into his tumultuous thoughts. Matthew a father? What would that mean? And could this make him so desperate that he … no, he just couldn't believe it. And Nicholas? No way. Ken? Robert had noticed his gloomy mood, and once he had overheard him talking to a friend on the phone, complaining about his wife's spending habits and their deteriorating relationship. Would he have wanted to make extra money by stealing and selling wine?

If Robert was honest with himself, he had to admit that he knew very little about his employees, or his family for that matter. He had always assumed everything was basically all right. He had been focusing on making his wine famous and left the people on the estate to their own devices. Obviously, that had been a mistake.

Chapter 25

Robert gazed out the living room window of his home. It was early in the morning, the sun showing its first rays on the horizon. He usually enjoyed the early morning hours when everything was still fresh. Now, however, a cloud of gloom and sadness hovered over the estate. He couldn't get the image of Romero's burning body and the pain and despair in Juanita's and Nora's eyes out of his mind. He had barely slept all night, thinking about the crisis with Matthew and the whole rest of it, wine theft and all.

Janice opened the kitchen door and brought him a cup of coffee he gratefully accepted. "How do you want your eggs," she asked.

"Not hungry," he muttered.

"Come on, Robert, you need to eat." Janice put her arm around him. "We need to carry on. This whole thing is a catastrophe, but it's not the end of the world."

Robert couldn't help a quick smile. His wife was always the down-to-earth voice in a crisis. "Okay," he said. "But no eggs for me, just some toast."

"Have you been able to talk to Matt?" she asked.

Robert groaned. "No, I tried last night, but he wasn't home. Besides, I was too upset and angry about this whole thing. We probably would've just yelled at each other." He gave Janice a pained look. "Honey, I don't know how to talk to Matt anymore."

Janice squeezed his arm lightly. "How about in a civil way without yelling at him? And how about listening to him. I mean really listening?"

Robert hesitated. "Am I really that bad?"

Janice chuckled. "There's definitely room for improvement, but I love you anyway. And besides, it's not all your fault. Matthew is too hotheaded himself. You know like father, like son."

"What are we going to do if he really is a father?" Robert asked with a sinking heart.

"We'll decide once we know for sure. We'll support him of course."

Robert nodded. "What about everything else? The wine theft and all that?"

"Robert, that you'll have to leave to David Lauer. He'll deal with it. Focus on your relationship with your son. Leave the rest to the authorities."

"And you don't think Matt is somehow involved? Lauer seems to consider him a suspect."

"Lauer doesn't know us that well, so in a way we're all suspects. But you know your son. He'd never do anything like this. And if you have doubts, then you really don't know Matt, which seems to be your problem to begin with."

"Am I such a lousy father, then?" Robert's voice gave out.

"No, not at all. You have always been a good father, but lately the business has taken over too much. You have to find a better balance."

Robert sighed. "I know."

"Well, it looks like you'll have a chance to deal with Matt." Janice motioned with her head to the window. Matthew was walking up the hill. He took the steps of the short stairs leading up to the house two at a time and seemed full of energy. "Try to listen. Don't blow it. Hothead." She patted his back.

"Yes, ma'am," Robert said with a touch of sarcasm.

Matthew knocked on the door and Janice went to open it. He came in and sniffed the air. "Smells like coffee." He ran a hand through his tousled hair.

"I'll get you a cup." Janice left the room.

The two men stood facing each other in silence for a while. Then Matthew cleared his throat. "Did you hear about the paternity thing?" he asked, lowering his eyes.

"Yes," Robert said in a matter-of-fact voice.

"Did Mom tell you?"

"That would've been less embarrassing. No, I had to hear it from Lauer." Robert tried to keep his rising anger in check.

"I'm sorry. I know I should've told you earlier. But I didn't want to worry you without knowing if it was true."

"Is that really the reason?" Robert said. "You could at least be honest." He watched as Matthew blushed.

"All right, if you want to know. I was afraid of your reaction ... of you putting me down again, calling me a failure."

"Calling you a failure?" Robert was shocked. "When have I ever called you a failure?"

"Not directly, not in so many words, but just ... the way you treat me." Matthew averted his eyes.

Robert exhaled deeply, then took another deep breath. "We obviously have a serious communication problem. We'll have to talk about this in detail. But for right now. I have never ever considered you a failure. If I had, I would've never asked you to take over the estate. And I wouldn't consider making you the manager now." He held up his hand when Matthew opened his mouth. "Wait."

Matthew stared at him stunned.

"Let's get this clear. I consider you a capable winemaker and vintner and future business owner. But at the same time, you still have a lot to learn, and I'm not going to coddle you just because you're my son. If I see you make a mistake, I'll let you know. That doesn't mean I'm always right, but I'm still the owner and have the last word."

"Okay, agreed." Matt sounded subdued.

"And, in case you don't know it. I love you. And I know I don't always show it, but it's the damned truth." He pulled Matthew close and hugged him briefly. He saw tears in his son's eyes.

Janice came into the room with a cup of coffee and handed it to Matthew. "You're okay?"

"Yes. Thanks for the coffee." Matthew took a sip.

"Now, before we talk about anything else. What's going on with your paternity case?" Robert asked.

"That's what I came to tell you. I got the results. Negative. I'm not the father." A huge smile spread across his face.

The mixture of tears in his eyes and the smile reminded Robert of Matthew as a child. He realized that his son was still very young and vulnerable. He shouldn't be so hard on him. "Wonderful," he said and hugged him again.

Matthew seemed almost embarrassed about his father's sudden display of compassion. "What's this thing about me being the manager?" he asked.

"I'm offering you the position, but I want you to take a couple of days to think about it," Robert said. "I want you to be sure. If you're not ready for it, that's okay. I wouldn't think any less of you. You can always take over at a later date, and in the meantime, I could hire someone from the outside. But if you accept, that would mean we'd have to work together even more closely." Robert chortled. "And I think we do need to find a way to stop fighting each other all the time."

Matthew nodded. "I agree, and I'm sorry—"

Robert put his hand on Matthew's shoulder. "No, no. We're both involved, and we're both at fault. But most importantly, we'll have to figure out who the frigging hell is responsible for Romero's death and the stolen wine."

Matthew shot him a cautionary glance. "Lauer said I was a suspect, too."

"I know. We all are. I just hope he'll come up with something concrete soon. He needs to check out Adam. I told him several times. His connection to George Winter bothers me."

"Let David Lauer do his job," Janice said. "For right now, I think, it's time to eat. Matthew, there's enough for all of us. And there is enough scrambled eggs, if you change your mind, Robert."

"Okay, I guess in the meantime, I got kind of hungry. Let's eat." Robert put his arm around Matthew's shoulders and they went into the dining room.

Chapter 26

Adam looked up from his computer as Robert entered the office. Robert's black eyes bored into him for a short moment, then he gave a quick nod and began a conversation with Ken. Adam's heartbeat sped up. He could never get used to the hostile look. It had started when Segantino found out about him being related to Uncle George, who, as Adam found out in the meantime, was Robert's enemy. And now that wine had been stolen, Uncle George was an obvious suspect and by association Adam was too. He had really enjoyed working here, but now it felt all wrong.

"I shouldn't really work here anymore." Adam said after Robert had left the office.

"Why? What's the matter?" Ken looked up from his work and stared at him.

"That investigator, Lauer or whatever his name is, just grilled me about my relationship to my uncle. You know, the man who supposedly lost his job because of Robert. I mean what do I have to do with this?"

Ken scrunched his forehead and faced Adam. "What exactly did he say?"

"He wanted to know if I had stolen the wine for my uncle. I mean, the nerve." Adam pushed the laptop away and got up. "He asked me about my alibi for the evening of the fire. Fortunately, I do have one. Otherwise, he might have dragged me off to jail."

Ken gave a quick smile. "Calm down. I was questioned as well and so were all the others who were present during the time. He grilled me about my financial situation, even made a remark about my family's spending habits. Pissed me off." Ken smirked and shook his head. "So don't take his questions too personal. We all feel strange after being questioned. I heard from Robert that Lauer is a tough, no-nonsense investigator, but he rarely gets it wrong. He prosecuted quite a few felons successfully. He could hardly believe you have anything to do with this."

"I'm not so sure," Adam mumbled.

"Anyway, I don't think you should quit now. In a few weeks, your school starts again. If you quit now, it might look more suspicious. Lauer might think you're running away because you feel guilty."

Adam shrugged. "You could be right."

"Besides, I need you here. We're almost done with the project, and you're doing great work," Ken said.

"Thanks. Okay, I'll stay, I guess."

"Thanks, Adam, I appreciate it." Ken gave him a warm smile.

A little later, Adam took his lunch break. He had brought a sandwich and planned to eat it outside. It was hot though, and he was looking for some shade when he saw Julietta and Nicholas walk up the hill. They waved at him. Julietta stopped and waited until he caught up with her.

"Are you having lunch?" she asked.

He nodded. "Yes, I'm looking for a shady place. It's really hot out."

"Let's go to the cellar. Matt started to set up some tables and chairs for the entertainment area. It's nice and cool there."

"Okay. Are you having lunch as well?"

"Yes. I'll get my sandwich and meet you there."

"Good. See you later." Adam walked the short path to the underground cellar and sat at one of the wooden tables. It was pleasantly cool inside but being alone gave him an uneasy feeling. Cellars tended to creep him out.

He was still thinking about the interview with Lauer, and it worried him. Ever since his talk with Robert, he had tried to distance himself from his uncle. He never mentioned him anymore around the estate. Now, he needed to do this even more. He actually had a decent relationship with Uncle George. He got along with him better than his father did. Now, whatever relationship he had with George had become a serious liability.

"Hi there, deep in thought?" Julietta sat down across from him.

Adam hadn't even heard her approach. He needed to stop daydreaming. "Well, I'm still upset about my meeting with that investigator."

"David Lauer?" Julietta asked.

"Yeah. He practically accused me of having stolen the wine. You know the bottle I said my uncle gave us."

"What?" Julietta stared at him. "That's crazy. Didn't your uncle give you the wine long before this all happened? Before the wine disappeared and before the fire?"

"Well, according to Lauer, the wine could've begun to disappear before they noticed," Adam said. "I remember Ken telling me there was a lot of shuffling around of wine bottles when they moved to the new storage facility. So it was kind of a mess."

"Yes, but what does this all have to do with you?" Julietta asked.

"Obviously, my uncle and your uncle aren't great buddies. So they may suspect that Uncle George was trying to get back at your uncle and hired me as the go-between?" Adam snorted. "Idiots."

"I agree. I don't think they seriously consider you, though. Everybody gets investigated."

"Yeah, well that's what Ken said, too. Still … remember when I first met Robert in the tasting room, he acted really weird when he read my last name?" Adam scrutinized Julietta. "Did he say anything to you about it, about me and my uncle?"

Julietta hesitated, then shook her head. "Not directly, but I, too, noticed that he was acting kind of funny."

Not directly? What does that mean? "Do *you* think I have anything to do with it?" Adam glared at Julietta.

She looked at him puzzled. "Of course not." She quickly lowered her eyes.

Adam crumbled the paper he had wrapped his sandwich in and tossed it into the trashcan. "Got to go back to work." He sounded harsher than he wanted to, but he was disappointed. Obviously Julietta didn't trust him either, and it hurt him. He got up and walked outside. Julietta rushed after him.

"Adam, don't let it get to you, please. Things will clear up. They'll find whoever did it."

"I hope," he grumbled and headed back to the office. On the way, he met Matthew, who waved at him.

"Hey, there, how is it going?" Matthew, who had been in a grumpy mood the past few weeks, seemed to be cheerful again. Adam liked him. He had noticed that Matthew and his father had a somewhat tense relationship. Robert's son was often at the receiving end of his impatient outbursts. Adam smiled. He could relate. Although Robert had never yelled at him, the sinister looks he gave him whenever they met made his ambivalent feelings toward Adam more than obvious.

Chapter 27

"Hi, Matt. What's up?" Nicholas shouted and waved at Matthew. Nicholas and Sofia were working at the winery, getting ready for the harvest. Nicholas laid down the rag he'd used to clean the outside of the wine press. He watched as his brother walked across the meadow toward them. Matthew seemed to be in good spirits. He smiled and there was a spring in his step, something Nicholas hadn't seen in his brother for a while.

"Hey, guys." Matthew took off his baseball cap and brushed a hand through his curly dark hair. "Busy?"

"Yes, but never too busy for you." Sofia hugged him. "How is it going?"

"Pretty good," Matthew said. "Pretty damned good, actually." He grinned, then tried to put on a serious face. "I actually feel almost guilty for my good mood, considering what's going on around here."

"Spit it out, bro. What's making you smile like the sun?" Nicholas asked.

"Well, the first good news. The paternity test came back negative." A smile spread across his face. "And that's a big burden off my back, as you can imagine."

"Wonderful. Great." Nicholas slapped him on the back. "You know who the father is? Just curious."

Matthew shook his head. "No. Marcia didn't say. I suspect it's the man she'd been involved with at the same time we were dating. Whoever it may be, I actually hope it works out for her. I don't particularly care for the woman anymore, but I'd feel sorry for the baby, if he or she had to grow up in unpleasant circumstances."

"Well, fortunately, that's not your problem anymore," Nicholas said. "But you said the 'first good news'. What's the second?"

"Well, I had a long talk with Dad."

Nicholas guffawed. "And that's the good news?"

"Yes. Believe it or not. For once, we had an amiable conversation. In fact, he was even compassionate … almost loving." Matthew gazed into the distance, as if he couldn't believe his father's changed behavior.

"Whoa. Amazing. Good for you." Nicholas smiled.

"Yeah. Of course, we'll still be yelling at each other. I don't think we'll turn into angels overnight. But he did offer me the position of manager, now that Romero … has passed."

"Congratulations. And, did you accept?" Sofia asked.

"He wants me to think it over. And, to be honest, as much as I appreciate the offer, and I'd love to be the manager, I'm not sure, I can swing it."

"Matt, you definitely can do it," Nicholas assured him. "You've worked with Romero for years. You know the ins and out of the job more than anybody else."

"Yes." Matthew shrugged. "But it would also mean I had to work more closely with Dad. And that will be a challenge, an additional one." He paused. "Although Dad seems to realize that we both must make more of an effort, that he doesn't feel it's just my problem. You know the miscommunication, or whatever you want to call it."

"I'm glad to hear that," Nicholas said. "It means he's aware that he has problems relating to other people, including his son. I'm sure you'll be able to work together."

"I got the feeling he let Romero pretty much do his own thing," Sofia said. "So, perhaps, you'll have more freedom to run the estate as well."

"I hope so." Matthew looked thoughtful. "But you know, as much as I welcome the opportunity, it makes me really sad that it's because of Romero dying. This just sucks."

"Yes, I know," Sofia said. "And I feel terrible about Juanita and Nora. I haven't seen them around. Are they still with Juanita's sister?"

Matthew nodded. "Yes. Dad told them they should stay on in their home. He even offered to let them live there without paying rent until their financial situation is straightened out. And he would reduce the rent so they could pay it comfortably. He also offered Juanita a job at the estate. You know, Ken always needs help with the accounting."

"That's very generous," Sofia said. "You know, Robert can be difficult to deal with sometimes, but he really does have a good heart."

Both Nicholas and Matthew nodded.

"Any news from Lauer?" Nicholas asked.

"No, not yet," Matthew said. "Anyway, I'm on a mini vacation for two days. Dad said to take some time off and think about his offer. So, since I can't just sit around, do you need any help?" He pointed at the crusher and the wine press.

"Oh, we can always use two more hands," Nicholas said. "Or four more." He motioned at Grandpa Martin, who came strolling up the steep path to the winery. He stopped in the middle, as if to catch his breath, then climbed the last few yards. Nicholas, watching him, felt a little stab in his heart. Although Martin was still in good shape for the most part, age did creep up on him. A few years before, he would have climbed the hill without stopping.

"Hey, Grandpa," Matthew called.

"Hi there, Matt. How's it going?" Martin measured Matthew with a probing look.

"Great. I've good news." Matthew told him about the result of the paternity test and of his father's offer to become the manager.

"Excellent. Congratulations." Martin gave a quick smile, then looked serious again. "I just wish it was for a different reason."

"Don't we all?" Nicholas said. "By the way, when is Romero's funeral?"

"Any day, now," Matthew said. "Dad helped organize it. I'll let you know the exact date and time soon. The family wants to wait for a few relatives of his from Mexico."

"Does he still have a lot of family in Mexico?" Sofia asked.

"Not too many. Both Juanita and Romero were born in the US, so most of their family members are here," Martin said.

He turned to Nicholas and Matthew. "I actually came here to help, of course." He pointed at the wine press. "But I also need some quick help from one of you strong and able-bodied men." He grinned. "I got some bags of natural fertilizer for Grandma's garden, and I need to carry them to where she can use them. I'm getting too old and doddery to do it by myself."

"No problem, Grandpa, I'll help," Nicholas said. "And no, you're not old and certainly not doddery." He turned to Sofia and Matthew. "I'll be back."

On the way to his home, Martin said, "I forgot to tell you guys. I ran into George Winter at Rite Aid downtown."

Nicholas looked at his grandfather surprised. "You're kidding me. I didn't know you knew him."

"I used to work with him when he still had his position at City Hall, you know getting permits and all that. That was before he was arrested for accepting bribes. He changed somewhat, at least in looks. He gained weight. He looked almost like a bum with his dirty T-shirt and baseball cap and the six-pack of beer."

"Did he recognize you?" Nicholas asked.

"I think he did. Our eyes met briefly, but he looked away immediately. He must not feel comfortable around any of the Segantinos." Martin chortled.

"How was he back then, when you worked with him?" Nicholas asked.

Martin shrugged. "Unpleasant, is all I can say. I never had any serious issues with him, but he came across as a know-it-all and there was always something fishy about him."

"I didn't realize he lived in Paso," Nicholas said.

"I don't think he does. He may have just been in the neighborhood."

"You know Adam, his nephew, works at the estate for the summer," Nicholas said.

Martin nodded. "Yes, and I know Robert isn't exactly happy about it. Of course, when Ken hired him, he had no idea about the connection."

"What worries us a little, Sofia and me, is that Julietta and Adam are dating," Nicholas said. "He strikes me as a nice and honest man, but you never know."

"Yes, and he's quite handsome." Martin raised an eyebrow. "No wonder Julietta likes him. Let's hope he didn't inherit his uncle's criminal tendencies."

Chapter 28

Robert scrunched his eyes as he and Janice stepped out of their home. Thick, dark clouds lined the horizon, an ominous sign for the upcoming grape harvest. Heavy rain could easily damage the fruit at this stage of ripeness. Robert hoped that the brisk breeze would chase away the clouds. They were on their way to pick up his parents for Romero's funeral. His sons, daughter-in-law, and her sister were driving by themselves.

The funeral was held in the small Catholic church downtown. Romero had been well-liked and quite a few people from the town as well as relatives and friends from all over, including cousins from Mexico, came to pay their respects.

At the church, Juanita and Nora, both pale and with red-rimmed eyes, sat next to the other family members in the first row of the pews. Robert and Janice went up to them, hugged Romero's wife and daughter, and greeted the other members of the family. More than once, Janice pressed her handkerchief to her eyes and Robert blinked away tears.

Almost all the workers from the Segantino estate were present. Robert was grateful they had come. He and Janice sat a little further back, next to Matthew, Nicholas, and Sofia. To Robert's surprise, Adam was present, sitting next to Julietta. He suspected he had come because of Julietta, since he hadn't known Romero that well. It was kind of him to pay his respects though. Robert tried not to think badly of him because of his uncle. Whenever he saw him though, he couldn't help feeling uneasy.

After music and prayers and a short but thoughtful sermon by the pastor, the ceremony was over. Robert and Matthew together with two of Romero's cousins were pallbearers and carried the coffin to the cemetery behind the chapel. After the coffin was lowered into the ground, Robert and Janice hugged Juanita and Nora. To see them so unhappy broke Robert's heart.

The family and a few close friends got together in a restaurant nearby for lunch. Robert had insisted on paying for the funeral expenses, the meal, and the flowers. At the restaurant, the atmosphere was subdued. The Guerrero and the Segantino families sat together. A few of the long-time employees and workers, who were present at the meal as well, gathered at a table next to the families. Robert and Janice tried hard to make everyone feel welcome and relaxed. Robert noticed though that it wasn't just sadness about the death of Romero, but a feeling of uncertainty, even suspicion and dread, that permeated the room. People talked with their neighbors in low voices.

Robert knew the reason. Romero hadn't died of natural causes. He was the victim of a crime, and nobody knew yet who was responsible for it. It could have been anybody among them. It could be a member of the Segantino family or one of the employees. Robert was certain that nobody in his family was responsible, but, as Lauer had pointed out, he wasn't the most objective judge in this respect.

Soon after the meal was over, people dispersed. Robert told Juanita once again he hoped she and Nora would stay on in their place. Juanita told him she believed they would, but she wanted some time to think about it. For the moment, she and Nora were staying with her sister. Robert nodded and hugged them. His heart was heavy, seeing them in such pain.

He felt a hand on his shoulder. Matthew gave him a quick smile. "Want to meet at the office to talk about … you know the next steps with the estate?"

"Don't you want to just relax today?" Robert asked.

"No, I want to get my mind off the whole sad story," Matthew said.

Robert checked his watch. "All right, I'll see you at the house in half an hour?"

"See you then." Matthew joined Nicholas, Sofia, and Julietta, who drove back together.

His parents and Janice would drive back with him. His mother gave him a hug. His father put his hand on his shoulder as they walked to the car. They didn't talk, there was no need. Robert was just grateful for having his parents to support him.

When Matthew entered his office, instead of offering him a seat, Robert pointed at the window.

"Come on, let's drive around the estate, check on the grapes." Robert got up and grabbed his sun hat that was lying on the desk. "In fact, let's walk. I haven't done that in a while."

Matthew looked surprised but followed his father into the kitchen where he got two small bottles of water out of the refrigerator and handed Matthew one.

"As a kid and then a young man, I used to do this with Dad," Robert said as they walked outside. "But then the estate got so big, we needed the jeep or the tractor to get around."

Matthew put on his baseball cap and the two of them walked along the nearest vineyard. Robert pointed at the field with the Merlot grapes. "One of the early grapes Dad planted, aside from the Italian varietals."

They stayed mostly in the shade of the row of oak trees. The threat of rain in the early morning had passed, the clouds on the horizon having dispersed, but the air was muggy. After about half an hour, they were both hot. Robert motioned at a bench along the way. They sat down and took a few sips of water. Robert took off his hat and wiped the sweat from his forehead. "I'm out of shape. I need to get more exercise."

"What's stopping you?" Matthew asked.

"Work in the office, too much traveling," Robert said with a sigh.

"Too much traveling? Oh, really? I would've never guessed," Matthew quipped.

Robert punched his arm. "Cut the sarcasm." Then he laughed. "Yeah, you're right. I have to cut back." He paused, then shrugged. "I think I got a little obsessed with all these contests."

Matthew was stunned that his father had admitted something he had always denied. He glanced at him and suppressed another sarcastic remark.

"As the new manager, you can take over some of the visits to our most important clients, Chicago, for instance." Robert put his hat back on. "I didn't ask Romero, because I knew he hated being away from his family."

"I wouldn't mind," Matthew said cautiously. "As long as it's visiting clients."

Robert nodded. "I understand. Next time we'll both go together to Chicago. I can introduce you to James and Sonny and you'll see how it works."

Matthew nodded. "Okay." It could be an interesting change, getting out of town once in a while.

Robert got up. "Let's walk to the end of this row and then go home. I think Mom is making a light dinner after our heavy lunch. You can eat with us."

"Thanks, you don't need to tell me twice. You know how little I enjoy cooking."

"You need a woman at home." Robert chuckled. "I guess I shouldn't say that after the disaster with Marcia."

Matthew grinned. "You got that right. I'm going to enjoy my freedom for a while."

They walked home in silence. In spite of the sad morning, Matthew felt strangely buoyed. His father was finally beginning to treat him not as some lackey he could yell at, but as an equal partner. He almost didn't trust the change in his dad but decided to enjoy it while it lasted.

Chapter 29

The beginning of the grape harvest at the Segantino estate tended to be a feverish affair, no matter how carefully planned everything had been. The machinery was ready, the fermentation tanks sterile, the hoses and all equipment cleaned and checked. The weather, however, was beyond human control. Fortunately, the climate in the area was quite stable, but still there were surprises. Rain was forecast for the day Sofia and Nicholas had planned to pick their Sangiovese grapes. Nicholas called the manager of the picking crew and begged him to come a day early. The picking crew, however, was booked that day for a different outfit. Nicholas appealed for help to his father and brother, who fortunately agreed to lend him part of their grape pickers, since they didn't need them that day.

"Thank God," Nicholas said and hugged Matthew. "I owe you one."

"Hey, no problem, bro, that's what family is for." Matthew slapped him on the back, then walked down the stairs from the tasting room into the winery, where a leaking hose required his attention. Matthew called one of the cellar rats and asked him to fix the hose. Cellar rats was a nickname for the junior employees at the bottom of the winemaking hierarchy. They did the grunt work such as shoveling and cleaning out the tanks and preparing the barrels. He rushed to check on one of the fermentation tanks and talked to another of the employees who worked on top of it, then disappeared into the cellar.

Robert, standing next to Nicholas, observed Matthew through the window that connected the tasting room with the winery. He chuckled. "I think he is finally learning how to delegate. A few months ago, he would've fixed the hose himself."

"See, you just have to be a little patient with him. He's learning. He's good." Nicholas said of his brother.

"Well, you know me, I'm not exactly the patient type." Robert gave a quick smile. "I guess that's something I have to learn."

"Any news from the investigator?" Nicholas asked.

"Not really. Lauer said they're focusing on finding out who those phony agents are, hoping to find the connection to whoever hired them. They're also still checking out the burned wine storage shed." Robert gave an exasperated groan. "I hope they find something, for Christ's sake. It's awful not knowing who is behind this whole scheme. Makes you distrust everyone."

Nicholas took a deep breath. "I know what you mean. Well, I'm off to get ready for tomorrow. Thanks again for helping us out with the pickers."

"No problem. If you need anything else, let me know," Robert said.

Nicholas, taking a last glance at his father's large winery with the fermentation tanks and rows of hoses, stepped outside. He watched the harvest activity for a while. Tractors and flatbed trucks were driving along the fields that were ready for picking. A slew of workers, women with colorful scarves around their heads or sun hats, men with hats or baseball caps, were walking along the rows of one of the grape fields. The busy activity was occasionally interrupted by laughter and calls to each other, mainly in Spanish.

Nicholas smiled. The grape harvest was the highpoint, the crowning event of a year's worth of hard work. It was an exciting and often nerve-racking time. Would all the grapes be picked and crushed in time? Would the weather cooperate? Often the work at his father's estate began in the early morning hours and lasted late into the night and this went on for weeks.

It was a little less hectic at Nicholas and Sofia's part of the estate, since they didn't have that many fields. At the same time, they had fewer employees to do all the work. During harvest time, however, there really was no separation between Robert's and Nicholas's estates. They all worked together as Segantinos, and the word "family" assumed a heightened meaning, the two estates becoming one. Grandparents, parents, children, and all their employees worked together toward a successful harvest.

Back at his winery, Nicholas, Sofia, and Grandpa Martin did a last check of the equipment and machinery. They had collected a sample of grapes from the entire Sangiovese field. Now, they crushed the grapes and tested the sugar content with a hydrometer. The process was called bunch sampling. The result was positive; the grapes were ready for picking. They gave each other high fives.

Nicholas wiped the sweat from his forehead. "I'm so grateful Dad lent us his picking crew. I wouldn't have been able to sleep, worrying about the possible rain."

Martin scanned the sky. "I don't think it's going to rain, but better safe than sorry."

In the evening, Grandma Maria and Janice cooked for the whole family, so "the kids could relax one last time," as Maria said. The meal was an annual harvest-eve tradition. The prospect of the following few days and weeks of work pushed the thoughts about the stolen wine and the tragedy of Romero's death aside for a while. At dinner, however, Robert lifted his glass of wine to the memory of his friend. He put his hand on Matthew's shoulder.

"Let's all help Matt. It's his first harvest as manager. And he'll do an excellent job."

Nicholas saw tears well up in his brother's eyes. "Hey, you're going to do great. And we'll all help."

Matthew smiled and lifted his glass. "To Romero and to all of us."

They all toasted each other.

The following day, Nicholas shot up when the alarm shrieked. He groaned, stretched, then crawled out of bed. It was still dark outside. Sofia's part of the bed was empty, but he wasn't surprised she'd gotten up before him. They both were always a little anxious the night before the first picking. Although everything was ready there could always be surprises at the last minute. Nicholas opened the door and gratefully inhaled the scent of fresh coffee. He heard the shower going, glanced inside the nursery and picked up a toy lying on the floor. Little Henry had spent the night with Grandma Maria and would stay with her during the day so he and Sofia didn't have to stop work to care for him.

Nicholas went into the kitchen and poured himself a cup of coffee. He sipped the dark strong brew and looked through the window. A strip of purple on the horizon promised another sunny day. He kissed Sofia as she stepped into the kitchen. "Thanks for the coffee." He took another sip and went to take a shower.

After a quick breakfast of cereal, fruit, and yogurt, they grabbed two bottles of water and their hats and walked the short path to the winery. Nicholas breathed a sigh of relief as he saw the workers of the picking crew waiting there. Most members of the crew were Latinos.

"*Hola, como estan?*" he greeted them. He shook hands with Jorge, their leader, whom he knew from an earlier harvest. "Gracias."

"*De nada.*" Jorge touched the brim of his baseball cap in greeting. "Okay. *Vamanos,*" he called to his helpers.

The workers spread out over the Sangiovese field and began to pick the grapes, putting them into plastic crates along the lanes of vines. They were experts, and the picking went fast. A few of them collected the full crates and dumped the fruit into larger containers that were then hoisted onto the flatbed truck Nicholas had parked next to the field the evening before.

Once the truck was full, Nicholas drove it to the winery, where other workers put the grapes onto a conveyor belt and checked them for spoiled or damaged fruit, removing anything unsuitable. Sofia, Julietta, and Grandpa Martin were standing at the end of the conveyor belt and gave the grapes one last glance before they were dropped into the crusher and destemmer.

Everything was well organized, the workers were experienced and fast, and a few hours later, the field was picked, the stems of the grapes removed, and the fruit crushed and dropped into the fermentation tank. After Nicholas added the yeast to get the fermentation going, the grapes would be left to sit for a week. Later, the extended fermentation would last about four to six weeks. Then the crushed grapes would be pressed, and the juice siphoned back into the tanks, where the fermentation continued.

The picking crew was invited for drinks and food Janice and Maria had prepared and catered. In the evening, after Nicholas and Sofia had dinner at their grandparents' house, they picked up little Henry, who was already asleep, and brought him home. Exhausted but happy after a successful day, they went to bed early. Everything had gone smoothly and the grapes in the fermentation tank were beginning their magical transformation into delicious Sangiovese wine.

Chapter 30

Robert stood on the patio of his home. Daylight was beginning to spread, and the air was still pleasantly cool. Sipping coffee, he noticed a car drive up to his property. It was David Lauer's green sedan. Eager to greet the investigator, who hopefully had some more information on the wine theft and, more importantly, on the arson, Robert walked across the lawn, meeting Lauer halfway.

"Good morning. You got some news?"

"Indeed, I do," Lauer said.

Robert motioned him to come inside. "Want some coffee? I've some ready in the kitchen."

"That would be great." Lauer gave a quick smile. "Sorry for being so early, but I have a full day ahead of me, and I wanted to give you the latest news."

"No problem. We're always up at the crack of dawn anyway." Robert went into the kitchen where Janice, still in her robe, was sipping coffee. "Lauer is here. He has news. Why don't you join us?"

"Let me put on some clothes. I'll be right with you." Janice hurried toward the bedroom.

Robert pressed the button on the espresso machine and poured two cups of coffee. He put them on a tray, grabbed a carton of Half & Half in the refrigerator and a cup of sugar. He carried the tray into his home office and put it on the coffee table. "Sit down," he told Lauer and pointed at the visitor's chairs behind the coffee table. He sat at his desk and looked at the man expectantly. "Let's wait until my wife joins us. She is as eager as I am to hear the news."

Lauer nodded, added some cream to his coffee and stirred it slowly. He took a sip, then got up as Janice entered. "Good morning, ma'am."

Always the gentleman, Robert thought, amused.

Janice shook hands with Lauer and sat down next to him, putting her coffee cup down. "All right. I hope you have some good news."

"Well, yes. We did make a breakthrough, finally." Lauer took another sip, then continued. "We found one of the phony agents that tried to sell the stolen wine. We had him in our focus because of a previous conviction for fraud. He admitted having gotten the wine from someone in order to sell it, but he claimed he didn't know the wine was stolen. Anyway, after interrogating him for a while, he agreed to a plea bargain. He named the person who hired him to sell the wine for a lighter sentence."

"Who was it? The guy who gave him the wine?" Robert could barely contain his impatience.

"Someone you know," Lauer said. "Your suspicions about George Winter were right on target. He was behind the whole thing."

Robert jumped up from his chair, almost knocking over his coffee cup. "I knew it. The bastard."

"But how is that possible?" Janice asked. "If George Winter stole the wine, how did he do it? We would have seen him on the property, wouldn't we? Even if he came at night, someone would've spotted him. This has been going on for many weeks."

Lauer nodded. "Well, he obviously didn't do it himself. Of course, we tried to get a hold of Winter, but he seems to have disappeared. There is a warrant out for his arrest. We'll get him, don't worry."

"So we still don't know how he got the wine." Robert rubbed his forehead.

"Obviously, someone with access to your estate and to the wine must have helped him."

Robert and Janice looked at each other. "But who?" Janice murmured.

"Adam." Robert checked his watch and began pacing the room. "It could only have been his nephew."

"Well, I don't know." Janice shook her head. "Adam has only worked here during the summer, but didn't the bottles go missing before that?"

Robert threw his hands in the air. "The first time we noticed that bottles disappeared was July and Adam worked here already." He felt his heart rate rise. "I never trusted that bastard."

"Well, we'll certainly question Adam, but it is by no means certain it was him," Lauer said. "Does he still work here?"

"Yes," Robert said. "But not for long."

Janice held up her hand. "Come on, Robert, we don't know—"

"Of course, we do. Who else could it be?" Robert continued to pace the room.

"Did he even have access to the storage room?" Janice asked.

"The keys are hanging in Ken's office. He could've taken them and gone back after work. Come on, Janice, it's obvious."

"No, it's not." Lauer got up. "You need to wait until we have evidence that he is involved. And for that I'll need to talk to him. Will he be at work today?"

"Yes, later this morning," Robert said.

"All right. Perhaps I can still catch him at home." Lauer glanced at his watch, then faced Robert. "In the meantime, hold your horses, don't do anything rash. Do not scare him away. I need to question him. Remember, people are innocent until proven guilty."

"Yeah. Yeah." Robert hurried toward the door, then turned back. "Thanks for the news, David."

"No problem," Lauer said.

Robert was on his way to the Accounting Department, then realized that it was too early. Nobody would be there yet. He turned around, just as Lauer was leaving.

"Try to calm your husband," he heard Lauer say to Janice.

"Fuck that," Robert muttered. He walked over to the winery, trying to get a hold of himself. It was George Winter after all. He was trying to beat Robert with his own weapons, obviously out of revenge. Stealing and selling his wine and probably making a nice profit. Well, that will be his last deed for a while. Back to prison for that bastard.

"Hey, Dad, what's the matter?" Matthew asked as he entered the winery.

"You're up early," Robert said. Ever since making Matthew the manager, his son who before hardly ever was on time, and if then with disheveled hair and bloodshot eyes, was the first one at the winery. *Just goes to show, give someone more responsibility and they perform better.*

"George Winter is behind the whole wine theft and sale and, I'm sure, behind the arson as well."

"What? How? Did Lauer tell you?" Matthew gaped at him.

"Yes. He was here just now," Robert said.

"Did they arrest him?" Matthew asked.

"Not yet. They can't find him, but they will. In the meantime, I want Adam off the property."

"Why? Is he involved?"

"George Winter couldn't have gotten the wine by himself. Who else could it be? Adam had perfect access to the keys for the winery and the storage room."

"But, Dad, you don't know for sure. What does Lauer say?"

Robert shrugged. "He's looking into it." He glanced over at the office building. "Got to talk to Ken."

Ken, who had just arrived, looked stunned as Robert burst into the office. "Good morning. What's the matter?"

"Where's Adam?" Robert barked. He tried to contain himself and lowered his voice. "Not in yet?"

Ken looked at his watch. "He should be here any minute. Why?"

"I want you to draw up a check for what we owe him. And then I want him fired," Robert said.

"Why?" Ken stared at him in shock.

Chapter 31

Robert walked to the window, then turned back to face Ken. "I just heard from the investigator that Adam's uncle is behind this wine theft and sale, and most likely behind the arson as well. Adam must have helped him."

"But … are you sure? It could've been someone else."

"Who?" Robert called out. "Don't you think it's too much of a coincidence that his uncle is the culprit and his nephew just happened to work here? Perfect arrangement, if you ask me. His uncle is known here. He couldn't have walked around the estate without anybody becoming suspicious. Nobody would suspect Adam though."

Ken hesitated. He wanted to defend Adam, but he had rarely seen Robert so angry. He'd better not upset him even more. "Well, I'm sorry to hear this. He did excellent work, and I took him for a really nice person."

"Well, yeah, not all criminals look like crooks. Most don't."

"I just …" Ken took a deep breath.

At that moment, the door opened, and Adam came inside.

"Hello," he said, then his eyes widened. He obviously sensed the tension in the room, and Robert's angry face left no doubt that something was brewing.

"I want you to pack your things. You're fired." Robert spoke in a quiet voice but with a threatening undertone.

"What? Why?" Adam stared at him, then looked at Ken helplessly. "What did I do?"

Robert glared at him. "Your uncle is responsible for the wine theft and the rest of it."

"What? Uncle George? … How?"

"Don't play innocent." Robert approached Adam, pointing an accusing finger at him. "You must have helped him. Did you also burn down the shed that killed Romero?"

Adam, his face pale, stepped back and bumped against his chair. He plopped down, then got up again. "This is totally crazy. I had no idea my uncle was behind this. I had nothing to do with it. And I certainly didn't burn down any sheds. You're out of your mind."

"I don't believe you," Robert said. "I don't want you here anymore. You're no longer welcome anywhere on my property."

"That's so unfair. You're accusing me of something I didn't do." Adam's voice cracked.

Robert waved him away and turned to Ken. "Make out the check for the work he's done." He stared at Adam again, as if he wanted to say something else. Instead, he stomped out of the office.

Ken felt sorry for Adam. "This is too bad. I don't know what to say." He picked up the check he had made out. He had added the hours until the end of the week, thinking Adam deserved some extra pay for the unfair treatment. "I'm sure things will clear up. I don't believe you're guilty." He handed Adam the check.

Adam looked at it, then at Ken. "Thank you. I'm sorry. I enjoyed working with you."

Ken nodded. "Likewise. You did excellent work. Once this is over with and you need a recommendation, let me know."

"Thanks." Adam snorted. "You'd get into trouble with His Highness. He's such a jerk." He shook his head. "But if this is true about my uncle, it's just horrible."

"Well, you can't control what members of your family do," Ken said. He sounded dejected.

"We're not close," Adam mumbled. "Our two families I mean." He walked toward the door.

"Again, thank you," Ken said. "And I've a feeling I'll see you again." He tried to sound hopeful.

Adam raised an eyebrow and shrugged. "Maybe." He gave a weak smile and left.

Outside, Adam ran into David Lauer. He stopped, anger surging through him about the unfair accusations. "So, you've come to arrest me? Make my day. It couldn't get any worse. I just got fired."

Lauer shook his head. "There's no reason for me to arrest you. Unless you have something to confess."

Adam stared at him. "Look, I have nothing to do with this. I'm as shocked to hear about my uncle as anybody."

"Who told you?" Lauer asked in a sharp tone.

"Segantino." Adam motioned with his head toward Ken's office.

"Robert?"

Adam nodded.

"Damn." Lauer's facial color deepened and he tensed his jaw. "I'm sure things will clear up. I'd like you to come to the station." Lauer checked his watch. "Shall we say in an hour?"

"You're sure you don't want to book me right now." Adam sneered. "I could skip the country." He was surprised that Lauer smiled.

"You're not going anywhere. The sooner we talk, the sooner this is over with."

"Am I really a suspect?" Adam tried to swallow a knot in his throat.

Lauer measured him with his penetrating eyes. "More like a person of interest. We're looking for your uncle. Perhaps you can shed some light on where he might be."

"I doubt it. As I said many times, we're not close. But I want to help in any way I can. I can't let that sit on me."

Lauer gave Adam a quick pat on the arm, then walked toward Ken's office.

Adam took a deep breath and tried to calm his nerves. He looked around, then began to walk toward Sofia and Nicholas's home, hoping that Julietta was there.

When he knocked on their door, he looked over his shoulder, afraid that Robert might have pursued him, but nobody was there.

Sofia opened the door. "Hi Adam. What's up?"

"You don't want to know," Adam said. "I just got fired. Robert thinks I had something to do with the wine theft … and the arson."

"What?" Sofia's eyes opened wide.

"Yep. I don't know if you heard. My uncle is behind the stolen wine, and I guess he is also responsible for selling it. At least that's what they told me."

"When did you hear this?" Sofia asked. Nicholas came to the door as well, looking at Adam, stunned. "Come on inside," Sofia said.

"Okay." Adam looked behind him again. "I probably shouldn't even be here. Robert banned me from his property."

"Well, this isn't his property," Nicholas said. "This is ours."

"Is Julietta here?" Adam hesitantly followed Nicholas inside.

Sofia shook her head. "No, she went to the college to buy some books. She should be back soon."

"Can you leave a message for her, please?" Adam asked.

Sofia motioned him to sit down but Adam remained standing. "Don't you want to talk to her yourself?"

"Maybe, it's better if we stay away from each other until this is cleared up," Adam said. "I don't want her to get into trouble by associating with a suspect."

"Are you a suspect?" Nicholas asked, frowning.

Adam gave a quick snort. "Not yet. Lauer called me a person of interest. He wants me to help him find my uncle. I really want to help, but I don't know Uncle George's whereabouts. Anyway, please tell Julietta I had nothing to do with it. I'll get in touch with her … once I'm in the clear."

Sofia put her hand on his arm. "We'll let her know. But please talk to her yourself. She'll be really upset hearing about this."

Adam nodded. "I will. Thanks. And I really don't have anything to do with it. I hope you believe me." He smiled briefly, then turned around, walked out the door and down the hill toward his car, his heart heavy.

Chapter 32

After Adam had left, Nicholas and Sofia stared at each other. "What a development," Nicholas said. "It was George Winter after all, Dad's enemy, who's behind this. We should've known."

"Do you think Adam is involved?" Sofia asked.

"God, I hope not. I don't think so ... I don't want to believe it, for Julietta's sake."

As if on cue, the door opened and Julietta rushed inside. She looked upset. "I just talked to Adam. I can't believe what's happening. He's so upset. Robert has no right to treat him this way." Julietta's voice shook.

"I know." Sofia put her arm around her. "I just hope this whole thing is cleared up soon. We have one big mess on this estate and now people are starting to accuse each other."

"I'm going to give Uncle Robert a piece of my mind. He's such an ... ass."

Nicholas screwed up his face. "Dad is always so short-tempered. I mean he has no proof that Adam is guilty." He stepped outside. "I can see Lauer's car next to Dad's house. Let's go and find out what's happening."

The three of them hurried along the path to Robert's place. As they approached, they heard Lauer shouting. The door to Robert's home office stood ajar.

"What are you doing, going around accusing people, threatening them? I'm the one who oversees this investigation. If I suspect someone, I'll do the questioning. What you're doing is interfering in the investigation. If you don't stop this nonsense, I won't share any news with you anymore."

A clearly subdued Robert answered. "I simply didn't want him on the estate anymore, so I fired him. That's my right."

"You did more than that. You told him that his uncle was behind this whole thing. That's information I gave you in confidence. And you go and accuse him of being his uncle's accomplice."

It was quiet for a few seconds. Nicholas, Sofia, and Julietta looked at each other. Nicholas was debating, if they should just wait until the altercation between the two men was over. At that moment, Matthew came walking into the house and gave them a questioning look. The discussion in the office continued.

"Don't you realize that was the one thing I didn't want to happen," Lauer said. "Let's say, you're right and Adam is his uncle's accomplice. Now, you just warned him. We don't know where Winter is. What prevents Adam from contacting him and scaring him off? Which makes our search for him more difficult. For all we know, he could already have left the state ... or the country."

"Well, obviously, I didn't think about that." Robert sounded defensive.

"That's what I mean. Why don't you think before you blow up?" Lauer spoke more calmly now but with stern authority.

Robert again. "Well, I'm sorry. Anything I can do to make this right?"

"Yes. Shut up. Don't do anything and leave the accusations to us."

"That will be a difficult task for my father," Matthew said with a chuckle as he pushed the door open all the way." Shutting up, I mean."

Nicholas wanted to laugh out loud at his brother's audacity. *Good for you. Tell him.*

Robert stared at Matthew angrily but didn't say anything. Lauer turned around and gave Matthew a stern look.

"Good that you're all here. What I told your father, also applies to you. Leave the investigation to us. That's our job and that's what we get paid for. If you hear or see anything alarming or suspicious, you tell me or one of my people, and nobody else. Is that understood?"

"Absolutely," Nicholas said.

"And another thing," Lauer continued. "We still don't know who collaborated with George Winter, but we know there was more than one person. They could be from the estate or from outside or both." He faced them with a stern expression. "Which means you are still under suspicion."

Nicholas took a deep breath. "You don't really think it's one of us here, do you?"

"What I think is secondary," Lauer said. "It's the evidence that counts. This is an ongoing investigation that goes beyond your estate. There are signs that we're dealing with a network of wine thieves. Anyway, I hope I made myself clear. You can always talk to me if you have questions or concerns. You all have my phone number and you can call me day or night. Okay?"

Nicholas nodded. "Okay."

"Adam didn't do it," Julietta burst out, her eyes flashing angrily at Robert. "You had no right to be so mean to him." Her voice cracked.

"I'm sorry, Julietta," Robert said. "I hope you're right about Adam. I still think he looks guilty."

Julietta opened her mouth, as if she wanted to protest. Lauer, however, touched her arm lightly. "How well do you know, Adam?"

Julietta glared at him defiantly. "He's my boyfriend."

"All right," Lauer said. "Why don't you come with me. You can help."

Julietta gave him a questioning look, then glanced at the others. "Okay."

"Let's talk outside." Lauer motioned to the door.

After they had left the room, Nicholas glanced at his father, who looked chastened. He felt it was kind of divine justice that the man who had a tendency to blow up and put others in their place, now got a taste of his own medicine, so to speak. At the same time, Nicholas felt sorry for him. He seemed to have aged. The pressure of the crimes, the death of his friend, and the general uncertainties had taken a toll on him. Nicholas went up to him. "You okay?"

Robert gave a quick grunt. "I guess I really screwed up. I just hope to God this case is soon over with or I'm going to crack."

"*Calma, calma.*" Nicholas patted his father's shoulder. "Just do what Lauer says."

"And get that fiery Italian temper under control." Matthew chortled.

"Oh, shush." Robert shook his head but gave a quick grin.

Chapter 33

David Lauer and Julietta were standing outside Robert and Janice's home. "How long have you known Adam?"

"I met him at college. He was at the same lecture as me. We're in the same program." Julietta thought back to the time she first noticed the handsome, funny man in a lecture on the history of architecture. "That was during the spring term … I guess since April."

"Did he ever mention his uncle? Have you ever met him?" Lauer measured her with his sharp gray eyes.

"He never talked about him until that day we met him by accident at the free concert in August, down at the park in Paso."

"How did you meet him?" Lauer asked.

Julietta told him that he had suddenly showed up and talked to them, that Adam had introduced him. "He gave me the creeps."

"How so?"

Julietta shrugged. "He was just an unpleasant fellow, he leered at me. He smelled of alcohol."

Lauer nodded. "Did you have the feeling he and Adam were close?"

"No. Adam said Uncle George and his father didn't get along. That George was the black sheep of the family. And, no, Adam didn't seem to be close to him."

"So, no indication that they might have a secret agreement, that they were working together?"

Julietta knew what Lauer was leading to. She shook her head. "No, no way. Adam wasn't involved."

Lauer gave a quick nod. "All right. I'm meeting with Adam at the station downtown." He checked his watch again. "In ten minutes. I'd like you to join us. We're trying to find his uncle who mysteriously disappeared. Perhaps you two can help us clarify where he might be."

Julietta hesitated. She didn't really know what she could contribute but she wanted to be present, even just for moral support for Adam. Lauer seemed to have read her mind. "Adam is pretty upset, and I think scared. He feels we suspect him. Perhaps when you're there, he'll be more relaxed and open up."

Julietta nodded. "Sure, if I can help."

"Okay, let's go." Lauer pointed his key at his car and unlocked the doors with a beep. They got in and Lauer drove the short distance to the police station."

"Do you work for the Paso Robles police?" Julietta asked.

"No. I'm from out of town, but they let me use an office at their facility for this case," Lauer explained.

When they arrived downtown, Lauer parked his car. Adam was waiting outside. His eyes opened wide when he saw Julietta. "What's going on? Is she a suspect, too?" Adam pressed his lips together and shot an angry look at Lauer.

"We're not talking suspects now," Lauer said. "I think that perhaps you can help us locate your uncle, and since Julietta met him once together with you at the park, she might think of something helpful."

Adam looked puzzled but shrugged. "Whatever."

"Let's go inside. You guys want any coffee, water?"

"Some water would be good," Adam said and Julietta nodded.

Lauer guided them to his office at the back of the station and asked them to sit. "Let me get the water." He left the room.

Adam turned to Julietta. "What's going on? Why did he bring us here?"

Julietta hugged him briefly. "Relax. I think he really hopes we can help him locate your uncle. He doesn't sound like he suspects you."

Lauer came back in with three small bottles of water and handed them two. He opened his own, took a sip, and sat down. "Okay, here is the thing. We're kind of stuck. Somehow your uncle must have gotten cold feet when he realized we were looking for him. He probably suspected that the whole thing was going to blow up in his face. So he ran. I've to admit, we haven't had any luck finding him."

Lauer turned to Adam. "We talked to your parents and they have no clue where he could be. Your father mentioned something about a cabin he used to go to, near Santa Margarita, that hiking and campground east of San Luis Obispo. And he said you were with him once as a kid."

Adam nodded. "Yes, that's true, but that was a long time ago. I was about six or seven years old." He wrinkled his forehead. "It was a small cabin not far from the lake where he used to go fishing. It's quite secluded. I was only there for a couple of days."

"I guess that would be a good place to hide," Lauer said, thoughtfully.

"I guess," Adam said, hesitantly. "Gee, I wish I remembered where it was exactly."

"Didn't your parents take you there?" Lauer asked.

"I don't think so." Adam paused. "No, Uncle George picked me up and brought me back. My parents knew that we were near Santa Margarita Lake, but I don't think they knew the exact location."

"And your parents let you stay with your uncle, despite of his less than stellar reputation?" Lauer raised an eyebrow.

"He was different at the time. He had a job with the government. He was married and had children. I guess my parents figured it was safe for me. Later, after George got in trouble with the law, my aunt divorced him, and the family moved away … hey, wouldn't Aunt Susan know where the cabin is?" Adam sounded eager. "Aunt Susan is his former wife."

"We already talked to her," Lauer said. She claims she doesn't know where it is. She'd never been to the cabin herself. She didn't sound very forthcoming. I guess they broke off any connection after George's legal troubles."

"I guess that's true." Adam spoke in a low voice. "The cabin seemed like more of a guy thing, those outings there. You know, pretty spartan, almost primitive. So I guess, it wasn't elegant enough for Aunt Susan." Adam gave a quick smile.

"What did the area near the cabin look like?" Julietta asked Adam.

"It was a beautiful place from what I remember, lots of hiking paths, a lake, lots of trees, mainly oaks, I think, lots of brush. It was kind of fun." Adam wrinkled his forehead. "Jesus, had I known that my uncle was a criminal, I wouldn't have enjoyed it that much."

"Well, people can change. Perhaps, he wasn't a bad person then," Julietta said.

"I remember he was already a boozer then. There was always a can of beer in his hand. I didn't think anything of it at the time, of course. I was too young. But in hindsight …"

"Okay, something else." Lauer stopped writing and glanced at them. He turned to Adam. "When was the last time you saw your uncle?"

Adam's forehead creased. He turned to Julietta. "It was during that concert in the park we went to."

Lauer nodded. "Julietta told me about that. And you didn't see him or have any contact with him after that?"

"No. That's the last time I heard of him."

"No phone calls? No text messages? No nothing?" Lauer's gray eyes seemed to bore into Adam. "I have to warn you that if there is anything you're withholding, perhaps to protect your uncle or your family, now is the time to tell me. If he approached you about the wine, if you gave him any kind of information, even if it sounded innocent, you have to tell me. Whatever happened, we'll find out. And it would be much better for you if you're upfront with me."

Adam's face turned red. "I told you everything. I only heard about my uncle being involved in any of this when Segantino threw it into my face and fired me. Jesus, everybody is accusing me."

Lauer raised his hand. "I'm not accusing you. I'm simply asking a question and giving you the information I would give to everyone in your position. You worked for Robert Segantino at a time when your uncle was committing fraud against him and perhaps worse. So, don't take this personally. I just have to ask."

"And I answered. I have no contact with him, and I don't want to have anything to do with the jerk anymore. Look what he caused? I've never felt so bad and humiliated in my life."

Julietta put her arm around him. "It's not your fault."

"Is there anything you can remember and want to add?" Lauer faced Julietta. "You only saw him that one time, yes?"

"Yes. No, I can't remember anything else." She paused. "Except he was clearly surprised that Adam worked for Robert. That I noticed." She looked at Adam, who nodded.

"All right, I think that's it. You've been very helpful. At least, we now have an additional area we could search." Lauer leaned back in his chair. "And, as I said before, if you hear or see anything or remember something, even if it doesn't sound important, let me know. You both have my phone number?"

Adam took his smartphone out of his pocket and checked it. "Yes, here it is." Julietta did the same.

Lauer got up and accompanied them to the door. "Do you need a ride back?" he asked Julietta.

"I'll take her back," Adam said.

"Good enough." Lauer smiled at them and waved them off.

After he went back inside, Julietta took a deep breath. "Well, that went okay. I really don't think he feels you have anything to do with this."

"I hope so. What about you?" Adam let his eyes linger on her.

"Of course not." She hugged him. He smiled and kissed her. They walked to his car arm in arm.

"You know," Adam said. "I really feel like checking out that area in the mountains. I can't remember where the cabin was, but I could at least try."

"You think that would be smart? I don't think Lauer would approve."

"Why not? I could help search. I really want my uncle to be found soon. The bastard. He's guilty not just for the wine theft and all that, but he may have burned down that shed that killed Romero."

Julietta nodded. "We could try. It could just be an outing."

"We?" Adam looked at her inquisitively.

"I'm not going to let you go by yourself. No way. I'm coming along. Besides, I've never been to those mountains and the Los Padres National forest, and I heard it was beautiful."

"Well, then, what are we waiting for?" Adam kissed her again.

Chapter 34

Julietta and Adam had been walking through the town and the nearby oak forest toward the lake for about an hour while Adam was trying to familiarize himself with the landscape he hadn't seen since childhood. They had left the car parked in town, since much of the hiking and leisure area was closed to traffic. It was a weekday and the place wasn't crowded. They met a few hikers, but most of the vacationers seemed to be back at work.

"Some of it looks familiar." Adam lifted his hand to shield his eyes from the sun and scanned the landscape. "There are areas I seem to recognize. Let's walk along the lake. I think we'd have the best chance of finding the cabin. I remember it was close to the lake but hidden behind trees."

"You said he came here to fish," Julietta remarked. "Was that in the lake or a stream?"

"The lake." Adam stopped short. "That looks familiar." He pointed at a group of oaks and a boat landing place. "Or not? Well, let's go and check it out."

They walked slowly along the lake. It was early in the morning, but it was already hot, and the sun was beating down. There was some welcome shade under the trees, and a light but pleasant breeze was coming from the water. Julietta took off her sun hat, wiped her forehead, and drank a sip of water from her bottle. Adam was walking ahead, then stopped.

"Let's walk more under the trees." He, too, took a sip of water. "I know the cabin wasn't that close to the lake."

They moved back from the water and walked among the trees for a while. Adam stopped again and touched Julietta's arm. "I think that might be it." He pointed toward a small log cabin, hidden behind oak trees.

Julietta's heart began to beat faster as they slowly approached. It looked old and abandoned, more like a shack than a cabin. There was a shabby porch in front of it. Some of the logs in the wall had holes in them, and one side of the cabin was overgrown with ivy. Even in the daytime, it looked spooky.

"Seems like nobody is here." Adam sounded disappointed. Julietta, however, was relieved. They were, after all, pursuing a criminal, and she only realized now that they had no plan what to do if in fact they did find George Winter.

"Let's check this out." Adam walked up the two steps of the rickety wooden stairs that led to an equally unsafe porch that tilted to one side.

"Be careful." Julietta grabbed Adam's arm. "What if he's here? What are we going to do?"

"Confront him," Adam said in a stern tone. "I don't think he's here though. I'm not even sure it's the right cabin, although it does look familiar."

He carefully walked across the porch, which creaked with each step. Julietta held her breath as Adam pressed down the door handle. To her surprise, the door gave. Adam looked back and scanned the area, then carefully pushed the door open. "Uncle George?" he called in a low voice. There was no answer. "Anybody here?" he tried again. Still nothing.

They stepped inside, Julietta following Adam hesitantly. The creepy feeling she'd had when first meeting George was back.

The first thing they discovered was a backpack on the floor. There was also a coffee percolator on the stove and a half-empty coffee mug on the table next to a baseball cap. "This is Uncle George's cabin all right. That's the hat he was wearing the night of the concert." Adam touched the coffee pot. "Still a little warm. He must be here somewhere. He left the door unlocked. He can't be far. I can't believe we actually found him." He sounded excited.

Julietta, however, didn't feel that confident. Fear flooded her. "We should leave and let Lauer know." She grabbed her cell phone. "No connection, darn it. I'll try outside." She walked across the rickety porch and down the stairs. She still didn't see any bars on her cell phone. "What are we going to do?" she asked Adam who had followed her outside.

"Let's wait for a while. I'm sure he'll be back. We can hide behind those bushes there." He pointed at a couple of shrubs next to the house.

"Okay." Julietta hesitated. "I still think we should leave and call Lauer."

"Shh." Adam grabbed Julietta's arm. "Somebody's coming."

A few seconds later, George Winter stepped out from behind some trees, carrying what looked like a pile of firewood. He dropped the logs when he saw them, stared at them baffled, and put one hand into the pocket of his loose jeans. Then his expression changed from shock to anger. "What in hell are you doing here?" He looked around frantically. "Are you alone?"

"The police are looking for you, Uncle George," Adam said. "They know about you stealing and selling Segantino's wine. Did you also burn down the shed that killed his manager?"

"You're just a little bit too smart for your own good. Why can't you leave that to the cops? You had to come snooping. And now you and your sweetheart are in trouble." George pulled a gun from his pocket and pointed it at them. Julietta inhaled sharply. She felt she was going to faint.

"What are you going to do, Uncle George? Kill us and add murder to your crimes?" Adam tried to sound brave, but his voice trembled. "You made my life miserable. They think I collaborated with you. I was fired from my job and banned from the estate. All because of you."

George gave a vicious laugh. "Idiots. They'll eventually find out it wasn't you. They'll have to look a little closer to the estate to find my collaborator."

"Then who was it?" Adam asked.

"None of your business. You already know too much. Now, I'm sorry, kids. I'm not going to harm you, but I'll need you to be quiet until I've disappeared." He approached them, waving his gun. "In you go. Now."

Julietta could barely walk, her legs trembled so much. Adam took her arm and tried to sound reassuring. "Don't worry," he whispered. "He's a criminal, but I don't think he'll kill us." They walked up the two steps and made their way carefully across the slanting porch.

Inside the cabin, George grabbed some rope from the kitchen cabinet. He pointed the gun at Julietta and then at the wall. "Sit down over there."

Julietta, her knees trembling, sat on the floor next to the wall. George then pointed the gun at Adam. "Tie her hands behind her back."

"What?" Adam stared at him.

"Do what I tell you. Now." He lifted the gun and pointed it at Julietta again. "Or I'll shoot her."

"Stop it. I'll do it." Adam's voice cracked. He took the rope. "I'm sorry," he said to Julietta. I have to do it." He tied Julietta's hands behind her back but didn't tighten them very hard.

"That's not enough. Tie them so she won't be able to loosen them." With the gun still pointed at them, Winter checked the rope. "More." He yelled at Adam.

Adam pulled harder and Julietta flinched as the rope cut into her wrists. "I'm sorry," Adam whispered.

George checked the bindings again. "All right. Now sit down in the corner." He pointed the gun at Adam. Adam obeyed. George set the gun far enough away, so Adam couldn't reach it but close enough to get a hold of it himself. "Put your hands behind your back."

"Are you going to leave us here tied up? If nobody finds us, we'll die," Adam croaked.

"Shut up." George began to tie Adam's hands. "As soon as I'm gone, I'll let someone know where you are."

"Then, they'll find you … ouch, you're hurting me," Adam said.

"Stop being a baby. They won't find me. I have a disposable phone. They'll have no idea where I am."

After tying up Adam's hands, George also wrapped rope around their legs. Finally, he got up and checked the bindings again. He grabbed the gun, his backpack and baseball cap, and walked toward the door. "Sorry about that, Adam. I really didn't want to involve you or the young lady. It's your own fault for playing cops." He left and slammed the door.

"Damn it." Adam began to pull on the ropes. "I feel like such an idiot."

Julietta felt like crying, but she knew she needed to be strong and keep her wits about her. At least the dangerous crook was gone. "Do you think he'll let someone know where we are?"

"Probably. Uncle George is a miserable human being and a criminal. But I don't believe he wants our lives on his conscience … then again, does he even have a conscience?"

Chapter 35

"We've got to get out of here." Adam started to pull on the ropes. After what seemed like an eternity, he felt his bindings loosen somewhat. He had used an old trick he had read about in a detective novel. He had tried to keep his fists tight when his uncle had tied his wrists. When he released them, there was just a tiny bit more space between the skin and the rope. It still took him a while to loosen the rope, and his wrists burned like hell. Finally, one came loose, and he was able to pull off the other one. The ropes on his feet came off more easily.

Adam got up and searched for a pair of scissors but only found a knife in the kitchen cabinet. He cut open Julietta's bindings.

"Thank God," she said, rubbing her chaffed wrists. Adam did the same, then got up and rushed toward the door. "Where are you going?" she called after him.

"I don't want him to escape." Adam grabbed his cell phone, but still couldn't get a connection. "Let's follow him. Once we're closer to town, we may be able to call."

Julietta rushed after him. "How do you know where he went? He could be anywhere."

"He could only have gone to where the cars are parked." Adam continued to plunge ahead, dodging trees and brush and looking occasionally over his shoulder to make sure Julietta was keeping up.

"Let's stop and try Lauer again," she said. They stopped. "Still nothing, darn. He has a gun, Adam, what if he shoots us?"

"He won't," Adam said. "If he really wanted to kill us, he could've done it before."

They came to the last group of shrubs and trees. All of a sudden, Adam saw a flash of yellow through the foliage. George's baseball cap? He stopped and held up his hand to warn Julietta. They watched and listened. The yellow patch gave way to a figure, walking between the trees.

"It's him," Adam whispered, his voice hoarse. "I have to cut him off before he gets to the car. Try to call Lauer again."

"Adam." He heard Julietta's worried voice. Not paying attention, he raced parallel to the figure hidden in part behind tree trunks, overtaking the man and then trying to cut him off. "Stop," he yelled.

Then everything happened at once. Uncle George turned around, his face in shock, his gun pointed at Adam. The popping sound of a gunshot and a burning sensation in his right arm, immediately followed by the sound of another gunshot. *Julietta*, Adam wanted to scream, but everything went black.

Julietta stared in horror as she heard the shot and saw Adam fall, then heard another popping sound and saw his uncle drop to the ground. Several policemen appeared as if from nowhere. She rushed to Adam and knelt down. There was blood oozing from his right upper arm through his T-shirt. She called his name, sobbing.

"Let me check." A firm hand pushed her gently aside. David Lauer bent down. "Adam, can you hear me. Come on boy, talk to me."

Adam's eyes opened. "You?"

"Yes. Don't fall asleep. Help is coming. You need to stay with me." He pulled off his shirt, wrapped it around Adam's arm, and pressed on the wound, attempting to stem the bleeding.

Julietta took deep breaths, trying not to faint. "Is he going to be okay?"

"Yes." Lauer turned around and waved as sirens shrieked. "Come here," he called and pointed at Adam. As soon as the paramedics attended to Adam, Lauer got up and walked over to where Adam's uncle was lying. The medics quickly checked out Adam, put him on a gurney, and carried him to the ambulance.

"I want to go with him," Julietta said and one of the paramedics nodded. Julietta rushed after them, passing by Adam's uncle lying on the ground. Lauer seemed to be talking to him, so he must have been alive.

Before Julietta climbed into the emergency vehicle, she glanced back and saw the medics attending to Winter.

Adam opened his eyes and looked around the white room, then closed them against the bright light. He felt a hand on his forehead. It was cool and comforting. He opened his eyes again. Julietta smiled at him, though her eyes were a little puffy, as if she had cried. He was so relieved she wasn't hurt, and he almost felt guilty for enjoying the fact that she seemed worried about him. "Hello," he said. He tried to sit up, but a searing pain in his right arm brought his attention to the bandage on it.

"Just take it easy." A sturdy looking male nurse put his hand on Adam's shoulder, preventing him from sitting up.

Adam turned his head and saw a man in a white coat, who looked like a doctor, walk toward him. "How are you?" he asked Adam.

Adam nodded. "Okay, I guess. Glad to be alive."

The doctor, a young man with curly blond hair and sharp blue eyes, smiled. "You're a very lucky young fellow. It's only a flesh wound, no shattered bones or injured joints. You'll be quite sore for a while. You need to check in with your own doctor to make sure the wound is healing properly and there is no secondary infection."

"Thank you." Adam managed a quick smile, then flinched from the pain of moving his arm. "What about Uncle George?" He glanced at Julietta.

"David Lauer shot him. He's in the emergency room, but they think he'll survive."

"He'll end up in prison, then," Adam said. "I heard a second shot after I fell down, and I thought … I was so scared. I thought he'd shot you. You know this could've gone awfully wrong." His eyes filled with tears at the thought.

"You're right," a stern male voice said. Adam turned his head and stared into Lauer's penetrating gray eyes. His heart sank.

"What you two did was extremely stupid and dangerous. You put your own lives at risk by going after a criminal. And all that without letting me or the police know. And I told you many times to let me know if you saw or heard anything. Do you have a problem understanding simple instructions?"

"I'm sorry," Adam said. "I only wanted to check out the area where I thought Uncle George could've had his cabin. I wanted to help. As soon as we found the cabin, we tried to call you." Adam looked at Julietta.

She nodded emphatically. "Yes, I've tried several times, but our cell phones didn't get a connection."

"Why then didn't you leave and call from somewhere else?" Lauer asked.

"It's really my fault," Adam said. "Julietta told me several times we should do that. But I didn't want him to get away. I was so angry about what he did … and the way he made me look." He took a deep breath and touched his aching arm.

"We'll talk about this later." Lauer sounded gentler. "Right now, I want you to relax. I'm sorry about your uncle. I had no choice but to shoot him when he shot you. He was a threat to Julietta as well."

"You saved my life. Thank you." Adam felt a knot in his throat.

"George Winter told me before they brought him to the hospital that he didn't mean to hurt you," Lauer said. "He was shocked when he saw you and the gun went off. He said he was sorry. I told him you'd be okay. And just to put your mind at ease, he also told me that you had nothing to do with the wine theft and sale. Once he's able to talk, we'll find out more about the whole thing."

"Did he tell you who else was involved?" Julietta asked.

Lauer shook his head. "Not yet. He fainted before I could ask him."

"So, we still don't know?" Adam said.

"I have some very strong suspicions," Lauer said in a low voice. "And some evidence. I'm sure he'll confirm it, once I'm able to talk to him."

Julietta inhaled sharply. "Someone from the family? The estate?"

"Nobody from the family." Lauer put his hand on Adam's shoulder. "I want you to relax and we'll talk later. Right now, your parents are waiting outside."

As the investigator was leaving, Adam's mother and father came in. His mother, a slender tall woman with blond hair, rushed up to him and tried to hug him.

"Watch my arm," he begged.

She pulled back a little, gently touched his other arm and kissed him, then burst into tears. "My poor baby."

His father, a sturdy man with thick eyebrows and a scowl on his face was less comforting. "What in heaven are you doing, almost getting yourself killed? What were you thinking, chasing after that criminal?"

"Dad, I'm sorry. I'll explain later."

"Well, thank God you're alive." His father gently touched his shoulder.

Relieved at not having to hear a second round of admonitions, Adam gave into exhaustion. He closed his eyes.

Chapter 36

Robert and Janice were having a leisurely breakfast, relaxing before the next harvest work load. They had spent the day before with Janice's family in San Francisco and got home after midnight. Robert sipped his coffee, gazing out the window. The sky was clear, except for a narrow strip of haze on the horizon. Janice put the empty breakfast dishes on a tray and carried them to the kitchen. Robert got up and opened the door, inhaling the scent of dry grass and jasmine.

"Matt's coming," Robert said.

"Good," Janice called from the kitchen.

"Hey, Dad, Mom." Matthew sounded excited.

"Hi there. You're up early," Robert said.

"Well, with all the excitement around here, I woke up early."

"What excitement?" Robert asked.

Matthew grinned. "I guess you don't know yet what happened." He sat at the breakfast table.

Robert stared at him with puzzlement. "So, what happened?"

Janice came into the dining room, carrying a cup. "Coffee?"

"Thanks, Mom." Matthew took a sip.

"I can make you some breakfast," Janice said.

"That's okay, Mom. We'll go over to Grandpa and Grandma's. That's where the others are."

"Who? What's going on? Tell us finally. Spit it out, damn it."

"*Calma, calma.*" Matthew took another sip. "You want the short or the long version?"

"Oh, for heaven's sake. Any version. Just talk." Robert called out, irritated at Matthew's attempts at dramatization.

"Okay, here is the short version. Your archenemy, George Winter, was shot. He's in the hospital. David Lauer shot him, but not before George shot Adam in the arm. And before that he, I mean Winter, tied both Julietta and Adam up in his cabin, but Adam got them loose and they chased him through the woods and—"

"What the fuck are you talking about?" Robert got up and stared at Matthew.

"Robert. Language." Janice grabbed Matthew's arm. "Is Julietta okay?"

"Yes, everybody is okay … well, except for George who's in pretty bad condition from what I heard. If he survives, he'll end up in prison."

"When did all this happen?" Robert asked.

"Yesterday, when you and Mom were gone."

"And nobody thought of informing us? There are phones, you know," Robert said.

"Well, once we heard about it here, things got kind of hectic. We rushed to the hospital. Adam was injured and Julietta was there with him. By the time we got home, it was late, and you weren't home yet. We figured we'd let you know in the morning."

Robert threw up his hands. "Excuse me for being dense, but I don't understand a thing."

"Well, let's all go to Grandma and Grandpa's. You'll hear the whole story in detail."

They got up and headed for the door. On the way to his parents' home, Robert tried to get a more lucid story out of Matthew, but his son just waved dismissively. "Just wait,

Dad. By the way, you owe Adam an apology, a big one." Matthew pointed an accusing finger at Robert. "He definitely had nothing to do with the whole thing, and one of the reasons he was so eager to help find his uncle is because of the way you treated him."

When they arrived at his parents' house, Robert didn't even knock. He just opened the door and barged in, followed by Matthew and Janice.

"Can someone please tell me what happened here?" Robert stopped short when he looked around the living room. On the sofa, Adam, his arm in a sling, was sitting next to Julietta. Sofia and Nicholas were there as well.

"Well, hello to you, too, Robert." His father got up. "Coffee?"

"No, thanks, Dad." He stared at Adam. "You were shot?"

Adam nodded. "Just in the arm, a flesh wound. No biggie."

"What do you mean 'no biggie'? You could be dead. And Julietta. What in heaven?" Robert collapsed in a chair. "Sorry, I don't mean to yell. I'm just shocked. And Matthew here told an incoherent crazy story that doesn't make sense."

"Excuse me." Matthew lifted an eyebrow and grinned. "You mean, you didn't like my dramatic interpretation? I thought it was rather good myself."

Adam observed Robert closely. He seemed like a different man from the one that verbally attacked him days ago. He was still his impatient self, but his eyes no longer glared at him hatefully. In fact, he looked concerned. Adam glanced at Julietta. "Where to start?"

He began by saying that he was so shocked by what his uncle had done and how it reflected on him that he wanted to do whatever he could to help. He told them about his and

Julietta's talk with Lauer, his memories of the cabin his uncle had where he visited once as a boy. "So, we decided to just look around that area. I didn't really think we'd find the place or Uncle George, but we did."

After he finished the story, Robert who had been watching him intently, got up and paced around the room. "This is crazy. You could both be dead. Why didn't you call the police when you found the cabin?"

"We tried several times," Julietta said. "There was no service on our cell phones. We were too far away, I guess." She told him the rest of their adventure, how Adam got shot, how Lauer and the police appeared, and that George got shot as well. "David Lauer talked to him before they transported him to the emergency room," she said. "George told him that Adam had nothing to do with anything, he knew nothing about the theft or sale of the wine."

It was quiet in the room for a while. Then Robert walked over to Adam. "I guess I owe you an apology. I shouldn't have accused you without knowing all the facts. I treated you unfairly. I'm really sorry."

Adam looked at Robert's outstretched hand and his contrite expression. "It's okay," he said. "I can understand that you were suspicious of me. After all, he is my uncle." He smiled and shook Robert's hand.

"If you need your job back before school starts, it's yours again," Robert added. "And if you ever need a recommendation, let me know. Ken told me what an excellent job you did."

"Thanks," Adam said. "But college is starting in a week, and I'll be doing an internship next term. So, I'm good. But, yes, if I ever need a recommendation, I'll let you know."

Robert nodded thoughtfully. "This means we still don't know who worked with Winter. He couldn't have gotten all the bottles of wine from the estate without some internal help. That really bothers me. Who?"

Adam glanced at Julietta. "Didn't Lauer mention a suspicion he had?"

"Yes," Julietta said. "He told us that he had a strong suspicion and some evidence, too. He didn't say whom he suspected, but he said that it was nobody from the family. I was so relieved about that. He also said that once he was able to talk to Winter, he'd find out."

"That means it could only have been an employee?" Janice said. "But who?"

Robert rubbed his forehead. "Then it must be someone who had access to the keys to the storage facility and that excludes a lot of the short-time or new staff. And since it's nobody from the family, that leaves … Romero, Ken, and a few others." He hesitated. "Ken has not been himself lately … but no, I don't even want to go here. No more accusations without proof."

"Good decision," Martin said. "Let's wait for the investigator. No more running after criminals and getting yourself in danger." He shook his finger at Adam and Julietta.

"I gave her hell already," Sofia said.

"Ha. Ha. You're the right one to give someone hell for snooping." Nicholas laughed out loud. Everybody else chuckled, everybody except for Adam.

"What's that all about?" Adam wanted to know.

"Oh, you know, Julietta isn't the only one in the family who plays at sleuthing." Nicholas grinned. "My lovely wife here chased after our missing Great Uncle Angelo all the way through Italy last year. They were terrorized by some Italian thugs."

"Oh, don't exaggerate," Sofia said, blushing. "It was only the Piedmont. Don't listen to him," she said to Adam. "I'll tell you about it later."

Chapter 37

A knock on the door of Robert's office interrupted his brooding thoughts. He had been thinking about the disturbing incidences of the past few days, the ongoing uncertainty about George Winter's collaborator. As Robert wearily acknowledged the knocking, he noted that the day wasn't getting any more cheerful.

He got up and opened the door. A disheveled Juanita stood there, her face blotched and her eyes red from crying. "Mr. Segantino," she whispered with a trembling voice.

Robert hadn't been able to get her to call him by his first name, even after years of friendship. He attributed it to a somewhat old-fashioned sign of respect toward her husband's boss.

"What's the matter, Juanita?" He took her by the arm and led her inside. Her miserable face stung him and the pain of having lost his friend flared up again. He tried to hug her. "I'm so sorry," he said, probably for the thousandth time. "I know, I miss him, too. And I can only guess what a terrible time you and Nora are going through."

Juanita, however, stepped back and lifted her arms, avoiding his embrace. "No, Mr. Segantino. You don't understand." Now, she was sobbing bitterly.

"What is it, Juanita?" He was puzzled by her reaction. "You know you can talk to me about anything. I mean we're almost family, aren't we?"

Juanita shook her head. "You won't say that again after I tell you what I found out."

Robert's heart contracted. "Please sit down and tell me."

Juanita sat on a chair with a deep sigh. She pulled two sheets of paper and a cell phone out of her purse and gave them to him. "Romero wasn't the person you … or even I, thought he was."

Robert stared at the first sheet of paper. It was a list of amounts, some small, some quite large and dates next to them "What's this?" he asked, then looked at the second piece of paper. It was another list, this one of wines, bottles of Cabernet. A feeling of dread overcame Robert. "Where did you get this?" he asked.

"I found it when I was cleaning out some of Romero's stuff. That and the cell phone. One of the sheets of paper looks like a list of money he owed … to someone with whom he gambled. I had no idea he gambled. I don't know what to think. This is terrible."

She ran her hand through her disheveled hair. "Off and on, he used to get together with some of his friends for a beer or a glass of wine. They had been playing cards with each other for a long time. I didn't think anything of it. He needed to unwind and take a break from the pressure at home. I understood. He never came home drunk or anything. I didn't have any idea they were gambling.

"But now, I don't know what to think anymore. I don't know who my husband was anymore. We were so busy taking care of Nora, we didn't have that much time for each other. I mean …" She stopped. "But that's not the point. The second list … those bottles of wine. Are these the bottles that disappeared or were found in the burnt shed? And what does it all mean?" She covered her face with her hands, seemingly exhausted.

"Oh, Juanita. I don't know what it means either. I just have a terrible feeling. What about the cell phone?" His heart raced.

"I've never seen this phone before. It's not his regular cell phone. There are no recorded calls, but a bunch of text messages, seemingly from one of his friends, the one he gambled with. And Romero used his middle name. He signed his messages with 'Norman'." She pointed at the phone.

Robert perused the messages. The minute he saw the name of Romero's so-called friend, things started to fall into place, and Robert felt sick to his stomach.

"Juanita, I need to hand this over to the investigator," he said.

She nodded. "I know. This is awful. But I need to know the truth." Juanita broke down sobbing again.

Robert, equally distraught, got up, put a hand briefly on Juanita's trembling shoulder, and went to get his wife. Janice was doing some office work of her own for the charity organization she was part of. She looked up as Robert entered. Seeing his troubled expression, she got up.

"What's the matter?"

"Could you please come with me and take care of Juanita. She found out something terrible about Romero. She's in my office in tears. I need to call Lauer."

Janice stared at him. "What?"

"Please come. She'll explain it to you."

Janice followed him to his office where Juanita sat bent over, a bundle of misery. "Come on, Juanita, come with me, please." Janice helped the desperate woman get up and led her out of the office.

Robert sat down and stared at the pieces of evidence on the desk in front of him, his stomach in a knot. He grabbed the phone to call David Lauer. When he looked through the window, he saw the investigator walking from the driveway toward his home. Robert put the phone down and went out to meet him, his mind in a daze. Lauer greeted him with a quick wave.

"There are quite a few new developments," the investigator said. "Some which you already know, I assume. Adam and the young lady's search for George Winter and Winter being in the hospital. But there is more."

Robert nodded and invited him inside. "I probably know already what you're referring to."

"Oh?" Lauer examined him with narrowed eyes.

Robert pushed the cell phone and the two pieces of paper across his desk toward Lauer. "Juanita came to me in tears. She found this among Romero's things. She's totally heartbroken … and so am I."

Lauer picked up the pieces of evidence and nodded. "So she knows about it?"

"She just discovered this stuff while clearing out his things. How did *you* find out?" Robert motioned Lauer to sit down.

"I had my suspicions early on," the investigator said. "His pant legs soaked in gasoline which was used to burn down the shed. But I didn't have any conclusive evidence until recently."

"I still can't believe it," Robert said, rubbing his forehead. "Why? Why did he do it?" His voice trembled. "This is the biggest blow of the whole disaster."

"I know," Lauer said. "It hurts terribly to find out that a friend, someone you trusted, betrayed you. I'm sorry."

They were quiet for a moment. Robert felt increasingly sad and confused.

Lauer's voice interrupted his gloomy thoughts. "Is Mrs. Guerrero still here?"

"She may be. She's with my wife." Robert got up and entered the living room with Lauer following him. Janice came in from the kitchen, saying that Juanita had just left. She didn't want to leave Nora alone."

Lauer nodded. "I need to talk to her, but that can wait."

"Tell us the whole thing, please," Janice said. "What happened?"

Chapter 38

Robert, Janice, and David Lauer were sitting in the living room. Janice watched Robert quietly, his normally suntanned face was a grayish pale and his eyes had lost their luster. Janice was upset as well, but she knew how deeply he was affected by Romero's actions.

"You want some water?" Janice asked, glancing at Robert and Lauer.

"Yes, I can get it," Robert said.

Janice put her hand on his shoulder. "It's okay. I'll get it. I'll be right back." She went into the kitchen and brought back a tray with three glasses of water.

They all took a sip. Then Lauer cleared his throat. "We questioned Winter and some of his friends or associates as well as a neighbor of Winter's who overheard an argument between Winter and Romero. We also talked to a few people who knew Romero from years ago. Here's what we found out. Let's start from the beginning." He drank a sip of water.

"As a young man, Romero was a professional gambler for a while, and from what I heard, a successful one."

"What?" Robert stared at him. "Romero gambled? I had no idea."

Robert glanced at Janice. "That's news to me, too," Janice said. "Juanita certainly never mentioned it."

"I guess it was before he married, before he met Juanita. He may not have told her," Lauer said.

"Anyway, George Winter and a few of his friends had been playing cards for years. After he lost his job, went to prison and then got out, he joined them again. He then suggested they play for money. I think he tried all kinds of things to make money, with legal and illegal means. Some of his friends, however, weren't up for it. But one of them who stayed said he knew of someone who had gambled in the past. He might be interested. That person was Romero." He glanced at Robert.

"Romero joined them, and they played poker once a week, mainly for small amounts. When Romero introduced himself, he gave them only his middle name, Norman, obviously to hide his identity. He didn't want anyone else to know he was gambling again."

"I can't believe it. Romero led a double life." Robert paled even more. "He'd been somewhat secretive and aloof this past year. I wondered about it, but I thought it had to do with the problems in his family, with Nora, … but I would've never expected anything like this."

Janice was shocked as well. She was trying to think of any indication in his behavior that pointed to this.

Lauer continued. "Winter and his friends realized soon that they were playing with a pro, since he seemed to win all the time. Winter got frustrated, he obviously wasn't very good at gambling. He won some, then lost again.

"Winter confessed to me that one day he made an offer to Romero, or Norman as he was known to him," Lauer said. "Winter told Romero that since he was so good at playing, he wanted him to gamble for real. At first, Romero refused, but Winter handed him two thousand dollars in cash and told him to take it to a casino and play."

"That's nuts," Janice said.

Lauer nodded. "Yeah, well, it gets worse. I guess the temptation to dive into the world of gambling again, and without even having to use his own money, was too much for

Romero. You know, gambling can be as addictive as any drug."

Janice nodded. She felt dread rising in her. It sounded like the beginning of a nightmare.

Lauer continued. "Things went really well for a while, if you want to call it that. Romero won a lot of money, and Winter was excited. He kept giving Romero his share of the winnings and egged him on. But after a while, it all changed."

"Romero started to lose?" Robert asked.

"Yes, but there was a reason for it. Winter discovered Romero's real identity and the fact that he worked for you." Lauer looked at Robert. "He confronted him in a joking way, but Romero got scared. His cover blown, he wanted to stop, but Winter more or less blackmailed him into continuing, hinting that if he was found out, he would be in serious trouble. Winter promised they'd stop eventually but not yet. He became, or rather he already was, very greedy and didn't want to lose an opportunity to make extra cash. For Winter, Romero was the goose that laid the golden eggs. Unfortunately, his greed led to his and, of course, Romero's downfall."

Lauer took another sip of water. "One evening, after Romero started to lose, he lost thousands of dollars playing poker and blackjack, all of it Winter's money.

"Winter was distraught, of course, and blamed Romero. Romero stopped gambling and promised Winter he'd pay him back in installments. Winter, however, was impatient and came up with a plan, a really devious one." Lauer faced Robert.

"The wine scheme?" Robert whispered.

"Yes. See he was already involved in selling stolen wine from other outfits. The money he gave Romero to gamble with was from those illegal sales."

"The bastard. I can't believe this." Robert got up, walked around the room, then sat down again.

Lauer nodded. "So Winter hatched a plan to get back some of his losses. By putting pressure on Romero, threatening him with exposure, he could force him to steal wine to pay off his debt. But the most powerful motive for him was revenge. He admitted that much. He wanted to get back at you for what he believed you did to him."

Robert covered his face with his hands, then looked up. "I couldn't care less about the stolen wine. Corrupting one of my best friends, that's what really hurts me."

There was an oppressive silence in the room.

"Did Romero know yours and Winter's background?" Lauer asked after a while. "Did he know you had caused his arrest?"

Robert scratched his head. "I don't think so ... well, I don't know. A couple of other vintners and I hired a private investigator, but we kept it secret. Once it was clear, he accepted bribes and was convicted, I may have mentioned it, but not necessarily told Romero ... now I remember. Romero was away during that time. He took a leave of absence because it was then that Nora was diagnosed with MS. They took her to a special clinic and doctor in Mexico, some kind of alternative medical outfit. They stayed there for several weeks. It didn't help much though, so they came back." He glanced at Janice. "I'm sure I told him about the case, but I may not have mentioned George Winter by name."

"I just wondered if he would've agreed to play with Winter, had he known," Lauer said.

"I couldn't imagine he would've done so," Janice said.

Robert shrugged. "I don't think so either, but then I don't know what to believe anymore."

"Well, he may not have known in the beginning, but he found out, of course," Lauer said. "And by then, he was too deeply involved. He couldn't get out anymore."

"He could have gotten out," Robert said, his voice rising. "Why didn't he tell me? I would've lent him the money to pay Winter back. And even after he began to steal … if he had confessed, I may have forced him to get treatment for his addiction, but I wouldn't have fired him or hurt him. Jesus."

"He was a very private and proud man," Janice said. "I bet he was deeply ashamed and afraid his family would find out."

"I know, but still …." Robert shook his head. "Why? And why didn't I notice something was wrong all these months?"

"Don't blame yourself," Lauer said. "Remember not even his wife knew about it. He kept it to himself and it must have been a terrible burden. I don't think he was a bad person. He had an addiction he thought he'd overcome. He got caught in a web of lies and deceit. He was weak, and he got hurt by a devious and hateful person that I hope to put behind bars for many years."

Robert looked up. "I hope so, too."

"The saddest part is that it won't bring Romero back," Janice said. Her eyes filled with tears as she thought about the pain and shame that his and Winter's actions had brought for his wife and daughter.

Chapter 39

It was early morning, still cool enough for a pleasant walk outside before the September heat developed its full force. Robert was walking along one of his vineyards. He had begun to walk and exercise more again, leaving the car behind. He saw Matthew drive a Jeep along the extensive vineyards toward the field with the Syrah grapes, one of the last ones to be harvested. His son lifted his hand and waved, and Robert acknowledged him with a quick wave back and a forced smile. These days, he could barely conjure up any kind of enthusiasm for his estate and the harvest. The troubling and upsetting development of the wine theft and sale and the betrayal by Romero, whom he had considered a close and loyal friend, left a dark cloud over everything Robert did and thought.

Soon it would be time for the yearly harvest festival, but Robert was in no mood to celebrate. He went through his daily tasks almost automatically. He tried to feel inspired but to no avail. He was grateful for a rich harvest and for the fact that the period of uncertainties was over, but he was deeply unhappy about the outcome.

After a short walk along the edge of one of his fields, he sat on a wooden bench under one of the oak trees. His gaze fell on the meadows with the yellow and brown grass, burnt by the summer sun and dotted with dark green oaks next to the symmetrical rows of vines that stretched over the hills and valleys. In the past, the view of his vast estate had filled him with pride and joy, but today he felt emotionally numb and empty. There was one question that kept coming up again and again: Why? Why hadn't Romero trusted him enough to ask for advice or help before it was too late? He had lived next to him, tangled in lies and deceit, and had never once approached him for help.

Robert was angry with Romero, not so much for having stolen the wine, but for betraying his trust and collaborating with his archenemy, George Winter, even if Romero may not have been aware of it at first. But once he was, why hadn't he stopped and confessed? Robert's anger, however, paled in comparison with the disappointment and sadness because of his friend's betrayal.

"A penny for your thoughts." The voice startled Robert. He looked up at Janice who had followed him to the bench. She sat down and hugged him.

Robert sighed. "I just can't figure it out."

"Figure out what?"

"That Romero didn't trust me, that he didn't admit he struggled with an addiction. I mean we've been friends for many years." Robert's voice broke. "But worse, that I didn't notice anything was wrong, I mean seriously wrong, with him."

"Nobody did, Robert, not even his wife."

"I know, but still…"

"Robert, you're asking yourself the wrong question. Romero was an intelligent adult man. He knew we loved him. He betrayed our trust. He was desperate, yes, and if he had confessed, we would've found it in our hearts to forgive him. But he didn't." She hugged him. "Stop blaming yourself."

"So, what's the right question then?" Robert asked. "You said I asked the wrong question."

Janice paused. "The question is, how do we go on from here? What's going to happen to Juanita and Nora now? Juanita said they wanted to move."

Robert gazed into the distance, then brought his eyes back and glanced at Janice. "I told them to stay, actually I begged them. I don't want to lose them as well. Nora was happy here, and I think once they gain their footing again, they'll be able to move on with life. But Juanita is still so ashamed. She said she'd feel bad living in the same house after all that happened."

"She may change her mind," Janice said. "I know that Nora wants to stay, she said so. We'll have to convince Juanita, but she'll need time to sort everything out. For the moment, they're staying with her sister."

Robert nodded. "I offered Juanita a job, taking care of some of the paperwork for the estate. I bet Ken and Matt would appreciate the help. And I really think they need the money. We'll see." He got up.

"I need to get away to clear my mind. I think I'll take a drive down to San Luis Obispo to visit Angelo and Miriam. I haven't seen them in a while."

"Sounds good," Janice said. "Why don't you invite them and Sandro for dinner on Sunday?"

"Okay, I will." Robert got up.

"Drive carefully. And don't come home too late." Her voice sounded concerned.

Robert gave her a questioning look. "Do I look that bad? Don't worry, I won't do anything stupid."

Janice gave him a hug and went back to the house. Robert walked to the driveway where his Jeep was parked."

Chapter 40

Robert drove south toward San Luis Obispo where Uncle Angelo lived with his wife Miriam and their adopted son, Sandro. Robert parked his car and walked up to his uncle's home, a modest house with a beautiful, well-kept garden in a quiet residential area of the city.

Uncle Angelo opened the front door, stepped onto the patio, and waved at Robert. He was in his sixties, of medium height with a trim body, unruly black hair streaked with gray, and penetrating black eyes. Like Robert he had inherited his looks from the Italian side of their family.

"Well, well, stranger," he greeted Robert with his deep gravelly voice.

Robert gave him a hug. "I know it's been much too long, but here I am."

Uncle Angelo waved at the garden chairs on the patio and Robert sat down. Miriam, Angelo's wife, came outside. She was an attractive, tall and slim woman with short blond hair and blue eyes. She was quite a bit younger than Angelo, in her forties. After greeting him, she left to pick up Sandro from school. Angelo brought out two glasses of lemonade and they sat quietly for a while. Robert let his eyes wander over the colorful summer bloom in Miriam's garden. Gardening was one of her passions, as Angelo told him. For the first time that day, Robert was able to relax a little, enjoying the peaceful atmosphere and the calm that exuded from his uncle.

Robert took a deep breath. "How is Sandro doing?"

"Really well," Angelo said, taking a sip of lemonade. "He gets good grades in school, loves it, and wants to become a soccer star and a professional guitar player and singer." Angelo chuckled.

"Wow, quite ambitious, the little guy," Robert said.

"Tell me about it," Angelo said, then faced Robert with his black, intensive eyes. He cleared his throat. "So, what's going on with you? You guys have had quite some upheavals."

"You can say that again." Robert's mood, which had improved in the joyful environment, plunged again. "Angelo, I feel like a complete failure." He propped his elbows on his knees and put his face into his hands.

"Want to talk about it?"

"Well, you know what happened with Romero, right?"

"Yes, Martin filled me in," Angelo said.

Robert told him how he felt guilty not having been more in touch with his family and friends, that he was so focused on his work he didn't even notice the heartache and trouble people close to him experienced.

"Why hadn't I become aware of Romero's problems? I attributed his increasingly gloomy demeanor to his worrying about Nora. He grew distant, kept making excuses why he didn't want us to get together after work, which we used to do before all the time. I often wanted to ask him why, but I never did. Now, it's too late."

Robert rubbed his forehead. "Had I known that Romero was struggling with an addiction to gambling and needed money, I may have prevented the worst from happening."

Angelo put his hand on Robert's shoulder. "Robert, you're too used to being in control. Romero isn't your fault. He suffered from an addiction and he was too proud to admit his illness. So, he ended up stealing from you instead of asking for help. You cannot help someone who doesn't know or admit they need help. I know all about that. Remember how many times your father, and even you, offered to help me when I was in trouble many years ago? I was too proud to even consider that I was in trouble."

"Still, people close to you offered to help you. I didn't even realize that people close to me needed help," Robert said. "There were things going on in my family that everybody knew about, except for me. I'm sure you heard about Matthew's paternity issue."

Angelo nodded. "Yes. Janice told Miriam."

"See, I didn't even know about it until Lauer, the investigator, told me. What kind of a father am I? Matt had been troubled for weeks, and I hadn't noticed. Instead, I've been short-tempered with him. No wonder he didn't want to confide in me."

His voice trembled. "And then there is Ken, my accountant. We've worked together many years, and I hadn't even realized he had problems with his wife, let alone he was going through a divorce. I know I neglected Janice as well. She has been a good sport about it. The other day, I noticed that Mom and Dad had aged. When did all that happen? How much else did I overlook? How much do I really know about my family, my friends, the people around me?

"Lately, I've been asking myself if I sold my soul to my business, to success, fame, and awards, and now the devil is reaping his benefits?" Robert's eyes welled up.

"Ah, Robert," Angelo patted him on the shoulder. "Now, you're being a little too hard on yourself. We all make mistakes. The important thing is to learn from them. So, relax about your business a little more and pay more attention to the humans around you."

Robert nodded and brushed a hand across his face. He looked up and saw Miriam and nine-year-old Sandro approaching. The young boy carried a backpack and balanced a soccer ball on his hand. He walked up to Angelo and hugged him, then smiled at Robert. "Hi, Robert."

"Hey, there, Sandro, how is it going? I heard you plan to become a famous soccer star and professional musician."

Sandro grinned, a little embarrassed, but then nodded vigorously. "I'm going to start guitar lessons next week."

"That's great. Hey, perhaps you can play something for us during our entertainment evenings in the wine cellar."

"Okay, but I have to practice first," Sandro said with a serious face.

Robert laughed at the boy's eagerness. "I'm sure you'll learn it fast."

"Well," Miriam said, "first we have to concentrate on your homework, okay? Let's go and get a snack." She and Sandro went inside.

"You know you never told me how you found and adopted Sandro." Robert turned to Angelo.

"Well, you never asked," Angelo said.

Robert nodded. "See, that's what I mean. I'm just not aware enough what's going on around me, in my family. I'm sorry. But I really want to know."

"Okay, I'll tell you. "Want another drink?"

"No, thanks, I'm good," Robert said.

"Actually, I have a better idea." Angelo got up. "You know I work as a layperson for a Benedictine abbey, right? Have you ever been to one?"

"No, always wanted to, never made it. Another one of the things I kept postponing because of work."

"Let's go," Angelo said. "There are two facilities, one nearby and one in Big Sur. We'll visit the nearby one where I work. We'll come back here afterward. I hope you're having dinner with us."

"Thanks. Yes. That would be great."

Chapter 41

The Benedictine Monastery of the Risen Christ was situated in the backcountry of San Luis Obispo on a hill overlooking the valley below and the mountains in the distance. Robert parked his Jeep in the visitor's parking lot next to the chapel at the entrance to the forty-acre ranch. On the hill above them, he spotted a few monks in their long black robes. They disappeared behind the brush and trees that seemed to form a natural border between the private residence and the public area of the monastery.

Robert and Angelo stepped into the small chapel where they met a young monk, who sat on one of the chairs, meditating or praying. The interior of the chapel was simple. It contained a few religious pictures and a bookshelf with books and pamphlets. After looking around for a while, Angelo motioned to Robert to go outside, where they could talk without disturbing the monk's meditation.

Next to the chapel there were a few garden chairs. They sat down and gazed at the landscape in front of them.

"What's that down there?" Robert asked and pointed at a circular formation of stones.

"It's a labyrinth, which represents the fourteen Stations of the Cross," Angelo explained. "Monks and visitors use it to meditate. We can check it out later."

Robert took a deep breath and closed his eyes, savoring the moment of peace and quiet. They sat next to each other in silence for a while.

"You asked about Sandro?" Angelo mentioned.

"Yes. Please tell me," Robert said.

"I met him in a place similar to this in the Piedmont in Italy, in a Benedictine abbey in Moretta where I attended services as a lay monk," Angelo began in a low voice.

"I noticed a young boy hanging out with the monks and sometimes he sat in the abbot's office, drawing and painting. He was six years old. Abbot Francesco told me that the mother worked as a caretaker for a wealthy old man who had no family left. She and Sandro lived right next to the abbey, and the little boy often played on the monastery grounds. There was no mention of a father, so I assumed they were divorced or the father was dead."

Angelo stopped and gazed at the hills in the distance, thinking about that emotional time, which had been a true crossroad in his life.

"One day, one of the monks, who had played with Sandro, told me that the mother of the boy had developed an aggressive type of cancer. She died a few weeks later. I felt terrible for little Sandro and wondered what was going to happen to him.

"Shortly thereafter, Abbot Francesco called me into his office and told me that Sandro's mother had begged him to let Sandro stay at the monastery after her death. She had cut all connections to whatever relatives they still had in Sicily, and she really had nobody in the Piedmont who could take care of Sandro. She knew he felt comfortable here, and the monks were his best friends. She didn't want him to end up in an orphanage or with foster parents he didn't know. The abbot had promised to take care of Sandro."

Angelo paused, then continued. "He asked me to help him. The abbey wasn't really suited for a little boy. All the monks were adults. He needed children his own age. Abbot

Francesco felt that I could let him play soccer with the boys I counseled. He suggested I meet with him a few times a week, help him with his homework and let him play with some of the kids I mentored. Sandro loved to play soccer.

"I wasn't sure I was the right person to take care of him. I asked the abbot about Sandro's father and why he wasn't around. The abbot told me that his father had died when Sandro was three years old, under suspicious circumstances. He didn't tell me what the circumstances were. And now, at the age of only eight, he had lost his mother."

Angelo glanced at Robert. "I was struck by the similarities to my own past."

Robert frowned. "Similarities?"

Angelo gave him a questioning look. "Your father never told you the story?"

"I know that grandfather died when you were young, but Dad didn't give any details."

"Well, our father, your grandfather, died under equally suspicious circumstances when I was three years old. He was a crook and probably a mobster. And my mother passed away when I was eight. Just like Sandro's mom.

"So, I felt an immediate kinship with the little boy. But with my way of life, the possibility of having to run away again if my unsavory past caught up with me, I didn't feel I was a stable enough presence in Sandro's life. But the longer we hung around each other, the closer we became."

Angelo glanced at Robert. "Then miraculously Miriam came back into my life and soon after we began the process of adopting Angelo with the help of Abbot Francesco, who must have had some connections with the adoption agency. The process went amazingly quick." Angelo chuckled. "I suspect even the otherwise honorable abbot didn't shy away from using his worldly influence to speed things up."

Angelo shrugged. "That's the long and the short of it. The rest you know."

Robert had listened intently the whole time. Now, he briefly touched his uncle's arm. "Thank you for sharing that with me. It gives me hope. I think I screwed up a few things in my life, being too ambitious and constantly striving for more. The recent events brought me to an abrupt halt. I've been floundering ever since. I need to make some changes. I've been so lucky and blessed. It's time I gave something back. And I want to spend more time with my family."

Angelo put his hand on Robert's shoulder. "It's never too late."

Silence again, then Robert chuckled. "You know, Uncle Angelo, there was a time I called you a bum and no-good bastard. Now, I come to you for advice. You think that's a case of divine justice, karma, or something?"

"No, you were right, that's exactly what I was back then," Angelo said. "So, you see, if a no-good bastard and bum like me can turn his life around, you, a successful winemaker and vintner can do it, too, and much more."

They remained seated and gazed at the view of the rolling hills that stretched to the horizon.

"It's beautiful here," Robert whispered. "So peaceful."

"You could stay here for a few days," Angelo suggested. "They have some very comfortable accommodations for guests. The perfect place for peace and contemplation."

"I may just do that." Robert lifted a shoulder. "Though I'd probably go crazy in all this peace and serenity."

"You're right," Angelo said. "It's not easy. It takes getting used to being alone in a quiet environment, just with yourself for company, or, depending on your religious beliefs, with God or the universe. All kinds of unruly inner voices attack you. But if you stay with it, go through the turmoil, chances are, you'd feel renewed. That's at least what happened to me."

Chapter 42

Janice came back from a meeting of her community volunteer group. She put down her purse, poured a glass of water and drank it slowly, then got ready to prepare a pot of tea. She heard the door open; Robert walked into the kitchen and kissed her. Ever since visiting Angelo and Miriam, he seemed to be in a better mood again. He looked pensive but not troubled, a definite improvement. "I'm going to make tea. Want some?"

He nodded. "Sure. Thanks. How did your meeting go?"

"Okay," Janice said. "We're still looking for a piece of property for the planned youth center. You know the one the city agreed to support. But first we need the space. The land is just so expensive."

"I may have a solution for that."

"Oh?" Janice watched him surprised.

"I've been thinking," Robert continued. "About the business and all. There is a field close to downtown. The vines are old and need to be replaced. But then I've been thinking," he repeated.

"Thinking what, honey?" Janice smiled.

"What if I donated the field for the youth center? It's not as if we needed another vineyard. We can barely take care of the ones we have."

"You mean just give it away?" Janice looked at him startled.

"Yes. Why not? Of course, I'd have to consult with Matt and Nadia. They'd have to agree."

"Oh, Robert. This sounds wonderful. God, that would mean so much to the volunteer organization. Yes, of course, you'd have to discuss it with the kids. I bet they would agree. I think Matt sometimes gets overwhelmed with the whole thing."

Robert's eyes gleamed. In fact, he hadn't shown that much enthusiasm for anything in weeks, well really months, Janice thought.

"I was thinking of my friend Stephen Mason, the architect. He might be interested in doing the project, and I know he'd be willing to do it in an economical way. And didn't Adam say he needed to come up with a project for his master's thesis? Who knows he may be interested in working together with Stephen." Robert stopped and gave an embarrassed smile. "I'm probably getting ahead of myself."

Janice felt elated and she liked the way Robert's thinking was changing. "Honey, I love the idea. Perhaps, even Julietta may be able to contribute. She's still in the early stages of her studies but a little hands-on experience may really help her as well."

"You're right," Robert said. He rubbed his forehead, a gesture that usually showed he was either nervous or thinking heavily about a project. "There's another piece of property we need to decide what to do with. We'll either have to replant it or, I was thinking, we could sell it." He gave Janice an inquiring look. "Mark Llewellyn expressed an interest in it. He wants to plant a new varietal and thinks the soil and position of the field would be perfect. I thought we could sell it and give the money to the kids, to Matt, Nick, and Nadia. I know Nick could use the money to refinance the mortgage on the new house. Matt is still paying off his student loan. Of course the spendthrift should've done that before buying a sports car, but ... well, anyway. And Nadia could use the money as well once she's done with her studies … what do you think?"

Janice laughed happily. "It all sounds wonderful, Robert. What's gotten into you, though? I don't even recognize you anymore. What happened to good old frugal Robert Segantino, the relentless pursuer of success and yet another award?"

"Well, being frugal and driven has helped me become successful. But I think it's time to be a little more relaxed … and generous." Robert paused. "I guess what I learned from the whole debacle of the past year is how important family and friends are. Until now, I've always felt that a successful business and making as much money as possible is what I need to do for my family. But I think in the process I missed the most important factors." He shrugged. "Finding out what people think and feel, being close to them and listening … does this make sense?"

"It makes perfect sense." Janice felt tears rise. She was moved by Robert's generosity and new insights.

"But first of all." Robert hugged Janice. "I don't know how many times I've promised to take a real vacation with you, without thinking about the business. Now, we'll do it. How does a trip to Italy sound?"

"Wonderful. I'd love that. But we'll have to wait until after the harvest."

"Yes, I want to be around until the harvest is over with, in case Matt needs a hand," Robert said. "What about early next year? Julietta wants to go back home during the college break. We could go with her and visit her place in Vignaverde. We'll pay for her trip. She can be our tour guide. In fact, we could invite Adam along, if they're still together then."

"Wow, you're full of surprises." Janice chuckled. "I like that idea. Let's wait until next year. Give us some more time to plan. In the meantime, what's preventing us spending a couple of weeks somewhere nearby. There are plenty of wonderful vacation spots in the good old USA."

"A little love vacation, just the two of us. Sounds very romantic." Robert hugged and kissed her. It was a slow and intense kiss, interrupted only by the sound of footsteps. Matthew walked in and grinned. "Hey, guys, get a room."

"Oh, just the man I need to talk to." Robert let go of Janice. "What do you think of this plan?" He faced Matthew, then told him about his ideas of donating and selling pieces of land.

Matthew stared at his father, put his hand on Robert's forehead. "No fever. What happened? He must have lost the rest of his marbles."

Robert slapped his hand away. "Can you be serious for once?"

Matthew laughed. "I can't believe it. It's just … well, so unlike you. I mean you're thinking of downsizing? Giving away property?"

"We'll talk it through once Nadia is here. I don't want to do it without consulting with you. It's your future property."

"Well, you have my agreement right now. I think it's wonderful. I'm proud of you." Matthew slapped his father on the back.

Chapter 43

It was a cool but sunny day, the perfect weather for the harvest festival at the Segantino estate. In the early morning, however, Robert, Janice, Julietta, Adam, and Stephen, the architect, had a brief get-together to discuss the plans for the newly approved youth center in town. Stephen was a lively tall and slim man in his fifties, with curly reddish hair and green eyes.

Adam still couldn't believe his luck. He had the opportunity to work together with a well-known architect on the project. What was even more exciting, his professor had allowed him to use the work for his master's thesis.

Only a few weeks before, he had been fired from the estate, accused of collaborating with his criminal uncle. Now, he was part of the team, and Robert was treating him with respect.

Adam put his arm around Julietta, who was also present at the meeting, and gave her a gentle squeeze. Having her on the team was another lucky draw. It gave them the opportunity to work and spend a lot of time together.

After the introductions, Stephen told them a little about his former projects, one of them being a youth center for handicapped young people. He wanted to include facilities for handicapped youth and children in this project as well.

Adam was impressed with Stephen. They had met a few times before, and he had liked him immediately. He would have the opportunity to learn a lot from him. After the architect laid out his plans, he gave Adam and Julietta copies of it. He assigned Adam the task of designing a part of the inside and asked Julietta to come up with some ideas for the garden area. "I'll send you both the link to the online plans and we can exchange ideas over the Internet as well. But I'd like to schedule another meeting in person, to chat about what you've come up with. I think this is enough for the time being."

"Well, in that case, why don't you all join us for the harvest festival," Robert looked at his watch. "It should be starting about now. There is plenty of food and wine. We also organized taxi services, so you don't have to drive after enjoying our wine."

The group walked over to the underground cellar. Outside, tables laden with all kinds of delicacies, wine, and bottled water were prepared, awaiting the family members as well as the employees. Everybody who had in one way or the other contributed to the work was invited.

Inside the cellar, Matthew was overseeing the entertainment section. Here, too, were tables with food and wine, from sandwiches, seafood platters, salads, different kinds of breads donated by one of the bakeries in town, as well as bottles of wine, water, sodas, and lemonade. Up on the stage, someone from the jazz band tested out the microphone. Adam smiled as he saw his friend, Jonathan, the saxophone player. It was his band Matthew had hired to play at the harvest celebration.

He also spotted Ken, his former boss, who stood next to a few of the other employees of the estate. "Ken seems to be by himself. His wife isn't here?" Adam asked.

"They're separated. She left him for another man," Julietta said.

"Too bad," Adam said. "I feel sorry for him. He's such a nice guy, but when I worked for him I got the feeling there were problems with his wife, you know, from the way they talked on the phone."

"Yeah, it's kind of sad. They have two children. Another broken family."

Adam observed her, wondering if she was thinking about her own situation, having lost her father, who had had another wife back in California. "Well, let's enjoy the festival." He put his arm around her.

"Yes, let's join the family." Julietta motioned at the long table where the Segantinos were sitting. The grandparents, Robert and Janice, Nicholas, Matthew, Sofia, and a young woman he hadn't met yet were there. He assumed the girl was Matthew's and Nicholas's sister.

Robert introduced her to Adam. "This is Nadia. She just finished her studies and will be joining our work team soon."

Adam and Nadia shook hands. She was a tall, slim girl with blond hair and brown eyes. She resembled Nicholas more than Matthew. From what Julietta had told him, Martin and Maria, the grandparents, came from different European countries. Martin's mother immigrated from Italy and Maria's ancestors were of German origin. Robert and Matthew had clearly inherited the Italian features, both as far as their physical appearance and their temperament were concerned. The German influence, on the other hand, was more visible in Nicholas and Nadia.

"Yes, once Nadia works with us, there will be two of us," Matthew winked at Robert.

"You mean, two against one." Robert chuckled. "Not fair."

Matthew harrumphed. "Oh, I'm sure we'll all agree once in a while."

"Nadia will be the peacemaker, won't you, honey?" Janice put her arm around her daughter.

Nadia smiled. "Yeah, I'll try to keep the two hotheads in line."

Adam spotted Ken again, halfway across the room. He got up. "Excuse me for a minute, I'd like to say hello to my old boss."

"Ah, Ken," Robert said. "Tell him to come and sit with us."

"Okay, I will." Adam walked over to where Ken stood. They shook hands. Ken smiled. "Looks like you're no longer *persona non grata.*"

"Yeah, things have changed quite a bit. For the better." Adam smiled. "How are *you* doing?"

Ken shrugged. "Okay, under the circumstances."

"Sorry to hear about your separation," Adam said. "Julietta told me."

"Yeah, it's hard, but we felt it coming for a while. At least, we came to an agreement about the children."

"That's good. Robert said to come and sit with us." Adam turned around, just as Robert was approaching.

"Hey, Ken, come on over." He put his hand on Ken's shoulder and guided him to the table. Adam followed.

When everybody was seated, Robert gave a brief welcome speech, thanking everybody for their hard work.

"And talk about hard work," he said. "Thank you to my family for supporting us and, above all, I want to thank Matthew for doing an excellent job as new manager and organizing these festivities and, of course, revamping this old cellar."

Loud applause followed, and Matthew's face flushed.

Chapter 44

Not long after the wine festival, the Segantino family gathered in Maria and Martin's home for another celebration—Thanksgiving. Sofia and Nicholas had gotten up early that day to help their grandparents prepare the turkey spread. This year there would be additional guests. Little Henry was celebrating his first Thanksgiving. For the time being, however, he was deep asleep in the grandparents' bedroom. Great-uncle Angelo, Miriam, and Sandro, who had still lived in Italy this time last year, were present. And Julietta was also there, of course.

With that many people, everybody pitched in and brought dishes or drinks. Sofia and Julietta had baked the traditional pumpkin and pecan pies. Janice, happy that Nadia was home for the holiday, smiled brightly as she brought plates of vegetables and sweet potato casseroles the two had made together. Robert and Matthew had provided the wine and sodas. Maria and Martin were busy checking on the turkey in the oven, while Julietta was in charge of whipping the mashed potatoes and stirring the gravy. Nicholas would help Martin slice the bird.

Miriam, Angelo, and Sandro promised they'd provide the entertainment, meaning Sandro was going to perform his first songs on his new guitar.

Enticing smells came from the kitchen as Sofia arranged the buffet and added colorful paper napkins to the large dining room table.

Robert, who'd had to take care of some business in town, joined them just in time for the feast to begin. Before digging into the many delicious dishes, they did their yearly Thanksgiving tradition of each person naming something they were thankful for. It was, after all, a celebration of gratitude for what life had offered them.

Martin asked Robert to begin. Sofia observed her father-in-law, who had gone through so much upheaval during the year, trying to collect his thoughts. He cleared his throat.

"You know, this year has been a true eye-opener for me. It's been tough. I've lost a dear friend—I still consider Romero my friend, in spite of everything. In his admittedly crooked way, he made me aware of things. The most important lesson I learned—which I knew all along but had often forgotten …" He paused, looking around the table. "The thing I learned is how much I love my family and my friends and how important you all are to me. And I also learned how fast everything can come to an end, how fast you can lose someone. So, I'm grateful for a successful harvest, but most of all I'm grateful for my loved ones." His voice trembled a little, but he continued. "Matt and Janice were right. This whole running after rewards was getting ridiculous, and I'm done with it."

"Hear, hear!" Matthew lifted a glass of wine. "I, for one thing, am grateful for having a dad like you. Yes, we'll still be yelling at each other occasionally, but I'm really looking forward to working more closely with you."

They all toasted each other. Robert smiled and motioned at Sandro. "This young man here has been glancing at the table with the food. He's hungry."

Sandro blushed and grinned.

"I'm hungry, too," Robert continued. "Why don't we change the tradition a little and start eating. We can tell each other what we're grateful for while eating. What do you think?"

"Good idea," Martin said. "We don't want to let the turkey get cold."

They ate in silence for a while, then talked about what they were grateful for. The grandparents were thankful for their offspring, Matthew for not having to deal with any offspring yet, Nadia for having passed her exams and finishing her last term, Julietta for being able to help with the youth center. Nicholas and Sofia for the gift of their little boy and a successful harvest. When it was Janice's turn, she said she was grateful for her family and for her first grandchild. At that moment, crying was heard from the bedroom and Sofia got up to get Henry. They each hugged the little boy with the pudgy and flushed face. It didn't take him long to smile again.

"Where is Adam by the way?" Janice asked Julietta.

"He's having Thanksgiving with his parents, but I'll see him tomorrow."

After dinner, while everybody was drinking coffee and tea, Robert got up and pulled a few envelopes and a small wrapped box out of the briefcase he had brought with him. He cleared his throat.

"Well, as you know I had to take care of some business before coming here. Just wanted to let you know the piece of land is sold."

"Great to hear," Janice exclaimed. "So, it's all taken care of?"

"Yes," Robert said. "And here is the first payment from Mark Llewellyn. More will follow, of course." He handed the three envelopes to Nicholas, Matthew, and Nadia.

Sofia, sitting next to Nicholas while he opened the envelope, gasped when she saw the amount on the check. "Robert," she said. "I can't believe it."

Robert smiled. "Selling the land is part of trying to downsize a little. And I know that you have some debts you can pay off."

Nicholas stared at the check. "Dad, I … I don't know what to say. This is so generous and such a relief. We'll finally be able to refinance the house and lower our mortgage. This is a godsend. Thank you so much."

"Fifty thousand buckaroos, my God. I can finally get that second car." Matthew grinned.

Robert raised his eyebrows and shook his head.

"Just kidding, Dad. Of course, I'm going to pay off my student loan first. Thank you so much."

Nadia stared at the check in her hand as if in a trance. "What am I going to do with all this money? I've gotten so used to skimping while I was in college. I don't think I can handle it."

"Sure, you can, honey," Janice said. "Invest it. When you move back, you may need a down payment for a condo or house one day. Of course, you're more than welcome to live with us. There is enough room, but it'll come in handy for the future."

"Handy? I don't think that's the right expression, Mom," Nadia said. "This is such a surprise. Thank you, Dad." She got up and hugged him.

Robert seemed visibly moved by the expression of gratitude. He cleared his throat again. "Well, I have another small gift just for Matt. He seems to need it the most." He handed Matthew the small wrapped box.

"What's this?" Matthew said. "Another gift? This is more like Christmas than Thanksgiving." He tore open the wrapping and stared at the box, then burst out laughing, his face deeply flushed. "Dad, you're utterly impossible."

"What is it?" they all asked. Matthew handed Nicholas the box.

"Condoms. Extra strength." Nicholas grinned and held up the box. Everybody burst out laughing.

"What's that?" Sandro asked.

"Oh, my God," Nicholas said. "I forgot to take the tender ears of a nine-year old into consideration. It's just a joke. Have another piece of pie," he said, to distract Sandro's attention.

Sandro, however, looked at the box, read the label, and grinned. "Oh, I know what these are."

"You do?" Maria asked with a shocked voice. "Isn't he too young?"

Miriam shrugged. "Kids talk about these things. So we thought it was better to be honest about it when he asked."

"Can I have another piece of pie, then?" Sandro asked, obviously no longer interested in the delicate matter, to the visible relief of Grandma Maria.

"There is some left," she said, got up and went into the kitchen. She brought back a piece of pecan pie, topped with whipped cream. "Here you go, sweetie."

Angelo laughed. "He's a little manipulator."

Later, that evening, after the remaining food was cleared away and the kitchen, which had looked like a war zone from all the activity, was clean again, they were sitting in the living room next to the fireplace, sipping espresso and listening to Sandro sing and play guitar. They were all stunned by his beautiful voice and his quite accomplished playing. He played and sang a few Italian folk songs, some American country music, and ended with the first few verses of a song by Leonard Cohen, whom Angelo called his favorite singer and songwriter. Angelo, to the surprise of everyone, joined him with his dark, gravelly voice.

"Sandro, that was absolutely wonderful," Sofia said after they finished. "And I didn't know that Uncle Angelo could sing. I love Leonard Cohen's songs as well. You sound just like him."

"Well, not quite, but thanks for the compliment." Angelo chuckled.

"Yes, this is a perfect ending to a beautiful day," Miriam said. "But it's time for us to go home. Sandro has to get a few hours of sleep. He has a guitar lesson tomorrow morning."

"Well, Sandro, I hope you continue to practice," Grandpa Martin said. "Finally, we have an artist in our family, rather than just a bunch of winemakers."

Chapter 45

"I can't believe we're actually going," Adam said, all excited. He hugged Julietta. "I kind of feel like a freeloader."

It was a pleasant June day the following year as several members of the Segantino family gathered at the airport in San Luis Obispo. Robert, Janice, Julietta, and Adam were flying to Los Angeles and from there to Italy.

"No, you two are going to work for your vacation," Robert said. "You're going to show us around Florence and Vignaverde."

"Nice try, Robert." Adam chortled. "Julietta is the tour guide, but I'm still a freeloader. But you know, I'm very happy with my role. Getting a free vacation in beautiful Italy with my favorite girl." He kissed Julietta. "That's not something to sneeze at."

'I'm excited for sure," Janice said. "Finally, going on a vacation with my husband and getting to see Julietta and Sofia's vineyards in Tuscany. Can't get any better than that. I just wish the kids were coming along as well."

"Next time it's our turn," Nicholas said, bouncing little Henry on his hip.

"Yes, as soon as Henry is a few months older," Sofia said.

Robert slapped Matthew on the back. "Well, son, you're in charge now. No dad around to hassle you for three weeks."

"Oh, what a relief." Matthew wiggled his eyebrows. Then with a serious face. "But honestly, I'm kind of nervous. I hope no disaster happens."

"It won't. Come on, have a little more self-confidence." Robert grabbed him by the shoulder. "Besides, Nicholas, Sofia, and Nadia are here, if you need help."

"Yes, and don't count out your grandfather," Martin said. "I may be old, but I still know a little something about winemaking."

"Yes, you do, Dad. After all, we all learned it from you." Robert hugged his father. "Well, we better go to our gate," he said.

More hugging and kissing and then they were gone. Sofia felt somewhat melancholic as she watched her sister and Adam turn around once more and wave. She wished she could have gone with them.

Nicholas put his arm around her. "Don't be sad. We'll go next time."

At home, Matthew, Nadia, Sofia, and Nicholas spent the evening with their grandparents, enjoying the warm and pleasant weather on the patio.

"Oh." Matthew slapped his forehead. "I almost forgot to tell you. Juanita and Nora decided to stay after all, and Juanita will work for Dad together with Ken in the office. She insisted that part of her salary will go to pay us back for the stolen wine."

"That's good," Martin said. "She'll feel a little less guilty that way."

"Yes, but Dad told me he was putting the money into an account for Nora, without them knowing, of course."

"He's such a generous person," Sofia said. "He's changed a lot. I mean I think he's always been generous, but he's become … well, warmer, friendlier, a little less impatient."

"Yes, that's true. I think the whole disaster this year has changed him," Maria said. "For the better."

"Is it easier to work with him now?" Nicholas asked Matthew.

Matthew gave a quick smile. "He really tries, but of course he can't completely deny his personality. He still blows up occasionally but checks himself most of the time. One thing is for sure. He seems to appreciate me more." Matthew gazed at the others thoughtfully.

"That's great," Nicholas said. "But you know, you've changed, too. You've become more assertive and self-confident. I think he realizes that, and he likes it."

It was quiet for a while, and then a whimper came from the bedroom. Sofia got up to get Henry.

"Ah, the prince of the estate," Matthew said, laughing as she brought the little boy into the living-room.

Henry gave a quick squeal, as if to confirm his royal position.

The End

Acknowledgements

I would like to thank my friends and family for supporting me during the research and writing of this book. I'm very grateful to my editor, Linda Cassidy Lewis, for her detailed and careful editing and her many helpful suggestions. A heartfelt thank-you to Lisette Brodey, who did a final proofreading pass, and gave me additional pointers and suggestions. Thank you, too, dear Beta Readers for taking the time to read my manuscript, and above all thank you, Silvia Delorenzi, for your encouraging words. Last but not least, thank you again, Diane Busch, for designing a great cover. As part of my research, I read the fascinating book by Frances Dinkelspiel with the title *Tangled Vines* about one of California's most devastating arson fires that destroyed million dollars' worth of wine. It's a documentary but reads like a thriller. Much of my research about winemaking and the imaginary Segantino estate I did in Paso Robles, in particular at the winery of the Caparone family. The idea of the large underground wine cellar came to me when I visited the Eberle Winery. I truly appreciate the help of all the wine experts who have patiently answered my many questions. If I got something wrong about growing grapes and making wine, it is entirely my fault. I used Paso Robles and the Central Coast of California as basis for my story. However, all the actions and characters are completely fictional.

Christa Polkinhorn, originally from Switzerland, lives and works as writer and translator in the Los Angeles area in California. She divides her time between the United States and Switzerland and has strong ties to both countries. She is the author of seven novels and a collection of poems. Her travels and her interest in foreign cultures inform her work and her novels take place in several countries. Aside from writing and traveling, she is an avid reader and a lover of the arts, dark chocolate, and red wine. She can be reached by email at cpolkinhorn@msn.com or you can visit her at her website www.christa-polkinhorn.com.

www.ingramcontent.com/pod-product-compliance
Lightning Source LLC
Chambersburg PA
CBHW030639110726
47901CB00002B/499